July

July

Jeff Gutterman

SilverWind PUBLISHING

Cover photograph by Jeff Gutterman
Cover Design & Illustration by Lightbourne

The publisher wishes to thank Judy Berlinski, Gaelyn Larrick, Brian Paradis, Jill Hughes, Jerry Kalman, Tannis Lacroix, and Craig Upton for their professional assistance in the preparation of this book.

SilverWind Publishing, Los Angeles California

Printed in Canada
First Printing: March 1999
Second Printing: July 1999

Library of Congress Catalog Card Number: 99-93659
ISBN 1-893676-00-5

For Lovers Everywhere

Preface

Memories. Like dark threatening clouds hanging over the land you inhabit, silently moving across the mantel of your inner landscape, playing havoc with your neatly arranged thoughts, pushing their way into your world when you least expect or want them, immobilizing and paralyzing everything in their path. Memories.

The past. Coming at you at a speed difficult to comprehend, winding and twisting along the roads that have lain barren of movement for such a long time now, empty of feelings, emotion of even the slightest kind, long ago flung to its sides, out of direct visionary contact, flooding your mind with its all encompassing dimensions. The past.

Jeff Gutterman

The smile is prominent. It always appears first. And then, as if magically, before anything else takes its place, the passion returns, rushing into you, lifting that iron veil you placed between your heart and another's you had hoped to share with. A vision of everything right in your world. Of longing. To be there again. To be touched again by that special someone. To feel whole again. The inner you, reworked by another's touch. Instantly alive and feeling. Simply from remembering the smile.

The pictures. Moving over the screen of your mind. Separately. Together. In slow motion, to hold the mood without the chance of loss. Quickly, to grab the feeling before it disappears into those dark recesses again. Flowing smoothly, with occasional momentary rapid beating of the heart. To show you're still alive. Still willing to let the warm come in. The pictures.

In the incremental part of a second, a thousand replays of the one moment that meant the most to you. The illusionary space and invisible hand that moved your heart forever. The image of your feeling heart reflected back to you. Again and again.

July

I remember you. You've been a part of me from the moment of forever. And you've never left my heart. You've grown within me. Maybe beyond who you really are. Maybe who you really were to me. But it's you. Totally and completely. Your image, your smile, your laugh. Reaching out to me. Wanting me with you. Always.

K

July

There'll be times when the winds
appear to carry your dreams
far, far away.
But hold tight and stand firm.
For all life is a circle.
And even though the appearance
may create the illusion of a broken wing,
there remains connectiveness,
one part to the other.

Chapter One

It felt like it had been there an eternity, this bright yellowish sphere in the sky. Shooting fire from its soul, it expanded and flooded the windows with its light and well-being. With his back to the window, Wheeler could feel the warmth of its rays washing over his body. They penetrated his sweater, gently massaging his back and neck with their tender touch. That was the physical part. Strong, solid and unshakable. The spiritual part of Wheeler, his fragile inner sanctum, was also being touched by the background sounds. These gentle vibrations, carried on the wind that only seconds before had left their originating point as invisible strands of pulsating energy. They passed through the air unnoticed, arriving and regrouping at their invited destination. These waves of sound that encompassed everything within reach were now charged and changed back into their inception of voice and melody. And they moved through him, talking to every cell in his body, awakening his heart and making him smile ever so softly, knowing now that he could still be touched. It was a pleasant change from the previous week when the sky had roared and then split apart, releasing heaven's white spears and a torrent of rain showers almost everyday. For awhile that had put him in an ugly mood, but even then, when the clouds grew so thick that they covered the yellowish shell and allowed the darkness, Wheeler never thought about complaining. It's exactly what he had expected and wanted when he moved to the hill country six years ago.

He had needed to get away. From everything and everyone. Sam Wheeler's life had become dull and routine. He had moved through each day with doubt, longing for the night and the escape of sleep. It was the only true passion he had left. All his previous yearnings had slowly but deliberately taken their turn and walked out of his life. Little by little, Wheeler became a wizard at avoiding emotion and involvement.

But now it seemed something different was beginning to happen. Something very powerful. At first obscure, something was moving of its own accord, deep down in the well of his very soul. The sounds of the sparrows outside his window feeding their young, or the squabbling of the squirrels on the hillside attempting to change their family pecking order, wouldn't dissolve his inner thoughts, this voice within him. A gentle melody he thought he'd sealed and locked up for good, a long, long time ago. A big man, over six feet and then some, with a proportional weight, Wheeler's insides were almost healed. He tried to repress it. Not something he wanted to deal with just now. But it didn't matter. The wave of emotion was just too strong.

Her picture was returning. Not merely the overcast of black and white, but rather the reach right down and pull your heart out hue of living color. Her dark brown hair was the first thing that came into view, hanging gently on her shoulders, slightly curled at the bottom, trailing with an ever so slight tinge of golden when the sun would favor it. And then there was its spring-like bounce, moving through the air, lightly touching and again retreating from the friendly slope of her neck as she moved her head from side to side, all the while emoting first a pout and then laughter.

Jeff Gutterman

He could feel her eyes, dark green orbs that had easily surrounded him and with one giant tug had pulled him into her world with a slight tilt-of the-head look. Wheeler had always thought of her as magic. And now she was appearing from long ago.

Not too petite nor too ample, somewhere in the middle, all extensions from July's center seemingly able to return to her on silent command. His mind was racing now. The perfect match sexually. Never before had that happened. They had fit together as two independent streams of water, each melding into the other, cooperating, unifying. Over and over again. Easily, smoothly and quietly. His skin was dark and rugged, hers olive and smooth, longing to be touched, daring him to caress and stroke. And he had. Again and again. Softer than he had ever allowed his hands to follow contours of face and body. Slowly searching the exterior for the interior sensuality. And in a moment's sigh, both of them finding it.

Wheeler's look resembled a bull that had been caught and beaten, his sad expression finding several tears to cleanse his face. Sitting in his oversized stuffed chair remembering back, eyes closed, his heart moving through a vivid past, a movement without effort known only to him.

There was no other focus now. And somehow, some way, he knew she was receiving his thoughts and thinking back herself. For how could she not. This kind of spell happens only once in a lifetime and had them both locked in each other's thoughts. So he would tell himself.

With his fist slamming into the arm of his oversized chair, Wheeler seemed to brake his trance, got up and moved to the large picture window by the back of the house. Standing now, and once again appearing quite focused, the spell apparently hadn't been broken after all. He was moving in rhythm to his inner needs, crying out for more. Not just the memory but the real thing. He wanted to be able to tell her he loved her. Mostly he needed to hear the same from her. No more separation. The need, the desire, to find each other and get back together once more had a hold of him once again.

"I'm still not sure just what happened to you, what caused you to change, to back away. Why did you run away from me? From us? Where did you go? Where? Questions. A hundred questions that need answers. I have a need to know. A right to know," he shouted to the silence.

Wheeler had dropped to the floor on his knees.

"For the longest time I heard you crying out to me. But there was no voice, only feeling. July, where are you?"

The response was subtle and almost imperceptible. A light but yet constant scratching on the front door. The kind of persistence that weaves its way into your thoughts, as focused and pleasant as they might be. Was it something trying to get in or out, Wheeler thought. It didn't much matter. It was driving him nuts and he'd have to take care of it.

"Hold on, hold on, I'm coming."

When he opened the door he found himself staring down at a medium sized, sickly looking dog.

"Good God boy, you've got the wrong house."

Wheeler attempted to close the door, but the dog moved quickly through it to inside of the house, startling him. Once he was a good ten feet inside he stopped, turned and looked up at him.

"Now look . . ."

Sitting down, the dog kept his stare fixed on Wheeler. An eternity as they seemed to size each other up.

"Dakota. Fella is that you?"

The somewhat surprised recognition of Dakota by Wheeler caused the golden retriever to happily spring into him, throwing both of them into the front door.

If this was the past, Wheeler would have immediately started roughhousing with Dakota, but not now, not in the condition he saw his friend in. For now he just slid to the floor with him and stroked his coat. "My God, it is you. Where? How? I haven't seen you for almost a year now. I thought someone had taken you . . . God Dakota, you're a sight for sore eyes. Am I glad you're here again. And you know what? Maybe you're some kind of an omen. Maybe everything I lost will return to me."

————————————

Halfway across the country the yellow rays from the sky were also warming up the land beneath it. Sitting alone, a cup of hot tea in her hands and a rocking chair beneath her, was July. She was as beautiful as Wheeler remembered her. Moving gently back and forth she was also focused and reaching back. Wheeler. She could never forget him. How much she had loved him. How much they had loved each other. And still she had left, choosing this barren landscape as her home and life.

She remembered how it had started with Wheeler a long time ago. Her move from a small farming town in California's Santa Inez Valley to Los Angeles was the first step. Their meeting was the second. And then the love. Lots of love. And then misunderstanding. She had played a game of fantasy, of projection, and had allowed fear in. It wasn't that difficult. It was a part of her past and as such, almost impossible to quell. Beyond all her yearning, July had allowed the projection to guide and ultimately determine her fate. It had dominion over her feelings for the future of the relationship. It controlled her thoughts of Wheeler's feelings for her. She knew now that her mental forecasts were ill-warranted, but at that time they brought anger. And tears. And finally, separation. Months followed, she relocated and had thoughts of nothing but her and Wheeler. She wanted so bad to contact him, but she wouldn't allow herself to. Stubbornness, pride, fear and foolishness. And then the accident. A primal event unforeseen that caused her to misplace her memory for almost a year. A silent, temporary gift of sorts. But slowly, ever so slowly, the physical wounds healed and her memory of him, of them, began to return. Now the psychological pain was predominant again.

She wanted to see him so bad but realized that he had no knowledge of where she was, much less the accident. She knew that if he had gained an awareness of where she was and what had happened he'd be by her side. But she also knew that she had unwittingly backed herself into a self-imposed corner, granting her an overriding impression that all was lost.

As time passed she regained her sense of self, moving several times, trying to find a peace deep within herself, a calm that continued to elude her. But no matter the geographical location, her mind wouldn't release her emotions, wouldn't let her heal. If even for a short while her thoughts would move in other directions, they eventually returned to the two of them.

July lifted herself from where she had been sitting and headed back toward the house. Once inside she moved through a corridor of rooms toward the kitchen. A moment before pouring herself some more tea she set the cup down and glanced blankly out the wide divided window beyond the sink. Memories were hard to control and in a moment tears joined her thoughts in an all encompassing mood of resignation.

"What would you do if we found each other again Wheeler? Would the love still be there? Would it be the same? Maybe better? No, it doesn't get any better, does it? I'm going mad Wheeler. I just can't get you out of my mind. And no one else quite fits the bill. Tell me that you love me Sam. Even if it's only in my mind, it's what I need to hear."

The wind outside was starting to kick up a bit, moving the dust and broken weeds around the perimeter of the house to their new temporary locations. With the heat it was just too much. Out beyond the house was an old barn and just inside its doors was Darby. Quietly stretching her neck to the floor and then reaching into an adjacent stall, the mare was snatching as much loose hay as she could from one of the compact bundles that July had yet to break for her. She was beautiful and July was soon by her side stroking her head, leaning forehead to forehead as though they were one.

"You're the only one in my life that I'm sure loves me back. How'd you like to go for a ride girl?"

The saddle was only a stone's throw from Darby, but today July wanted to ride her bareback. Finding the bit and gently fitting her with it, July automatically threw herself up on her back, fastened her hands around the reins and with a gentle nudge of her boot, gave her friend her lead for the doorway. Quietly she moved from her stall through the barn to the outside, turned her neck toward July, neighed and took off.

It was just what she had needed. The mare had command. July had given her control. And Darby flew. Faster July thought, than they'd ever gone before. Stretching and reaching well beyond her normal gait. The richness of the moment with Darby put a smile on July's face. For the time being, Sam Wheeler had moved into that special compartment in the back of her mind once again.

Chapter Two

In the dead of winter one thing is certain. Everything moves slower. Old men and dogs think about where they want to go before the act of movement comes into being. Wheeler had some work to do but the mood wasn't moving him. A fire blazed less than a few feet from where Dakota was lying. The thin layer of skin that had hung over him when he had first returned home now gave the impression of a nice foundation of meat under it. And if expressions were all the communicative ability Dakota had available to him, you could tell he was happy.

Around the room were all the elements of an artist's life. Easels, some full, some empty.

Brushes and paints. Used pallets. And in the corner of one of the rooms sat a large unmarked canvas. Or so it appeared to the untrained eye. Sketched ever so lightly was an outline of July. No photographs to remind Wheeler. His memory was far more precise. Every now and then he'd glance toward the canvas, reach his hand to the top of his head, scratch it and turn away. He could only make it one dimensional. His mind would have to do the rest. And that just wasn't good enough. In a violent rage he threw the cup he had been drinking from against the fireplace, shattering it into hundreds of pieces before realizing he'd just scared the daylights out of Dakota.

"Oh boy, I'm sorry. Sometimes I just get so wrapped up in her memory. I've got to do something."

A quick glance around the room and Dakota knew a light had gone off inside Wheeler's head.

"I've got it. Ray Johnson has wanted those sketches of the wild horses for months now. Dakota, we're going to get them for him and take a trip in the process."

In the days that followed Wheeler was seen in town running from one store to another, gathering what he could from here and there. And every once in a while Dakota, always by his side, would look up at him and bark, causing a momentary slip in his gait as he realized that he'd forgotten something, turn and go back into the store he'd just come out from. He was gearing up for his trip and wanted to make sure nothing was left to chance. A large sleeping bag for himself and a smaller one for Dakota. There would be several nights they would spend on the open range to try and capture what they could under the light of the full moon. There would be no tent to protect them against an aggressive wind. And those nights he knew would be quite cold. Blankets. Plenty of blankets. Photographic equipment to capture a still image. Infrared film for the night and regular for the daytime. A tripod for stability and anchors to hold it in place if the horses were moving close and fast. The vibration alone could rattle your nerves. Pads to sketch with. Pencil, charcoal, to lay the foundation. Paints, colors of all hues to fit the pallet. And some new brushes. He would start and complete each painting with the horses. Nothing was going home with him unfinished. This was something he would complete and feel good about.

When the jeep that Wheeler called Stanley was full, the two of them jumped inside and headed back to the house to gather some additional odds and ends. By one o'clock in the morning Stanley was stocked full of all that would be needed. Everything practical. The memories, Wheeler told himself, would be left at the house.

If you could see tomorrow, you'd notice that several things have remained the same. Even in winter, the sun continues to rise in the east. And on a clear day, in a moderate sky, the intensity of the cloud cover will determine the moods of those below it.

July was situated on her roof, surrounded with a hammer and nails, a pair of scissors and a few sheets of tar-based roofing slats. She'd first visually inspect the area immediately around her and then feel it with her hands, eyes closed. Like an experienced surgeon, knowing when a bone was out of place by simple touch, July felt the hole before she saw it.

"Boy, you're a hell'va lot bigger than I thought you'd be. Feels like someone's started forging an entrance to a cave. It's a good thing I have enough sheeting to cover you up again."

Off on one of the corners of the roof, unseen but less than fifteen feet from July, two white doves softly landed and immediately began their mating dance. The cooing stopped July's activities and made her eyes search the skies around her for the sound. When she realized just where it was coming from she moved close enough to verify the sight and froze, tears filling her eyes as she turned her head and allowed her gaze to fall on the small birds.

They had nicknamed them Hamlet and Sunshine because of their personalities. Hamlet, a stone or two lighter then his mate, would dance around her, showing off by the constant up and down motion of his small, white bobbing neck. Sunshine, a tad or two brighter than Hamlet, would sit relaxed, moving her head from side to side with each up and down thrust that Hamlet would make. It was quite a sight.

Transfixed, July's unmasked madness allowed her soft voice to search for an answer. "How could you possibly be here? How? The last time I saw you guys was a light year ago, thousands of miles from here. Another time, another place. How? And why now? My heart feels like paper. This kind of touching can tear holes in its fabric."

Hamlet and Sunshine responded by moving ever so slowly toward July. When they were a whisper's distance from her, Sunshine again sat down, Hamlet dancing around her just once before moving onto July's leg. Now the tears were really filling her eyes, unable to see, only to reach out and touch Hamlet, a stroke accomplished with love of remembrance. The only voice she could find said it all.

"I don't understand?"

A response. An answer. To an open prayer. The gentle rolling clouds, feather weight to the wondering eye, floated ever so smoothly over the invisible current that made up the heavens. Hamlet and Sunshine began bobbing and cooing in a rhythmatic manner, forcing July to glance up at the imperceptible air stream that pushed and pulled the clouds in just such a way that they seemed to now surround a small hole in the sky. Through the hole a small, very powerful white golden light, filled the fringe of the clouds. It was like nothing she had ever seen. As she looked down on her two friends she noticed that the light hit them in just such a way that they seemed surrounded by the energy that radiated from its center. And as its power touched them, they seemed to lift into it and disappear.

"Gone. Without a trace. Almost like they'd never been here. Was I imagining all this?"

She was too focused on the sudden disappearance of her friends. Without warning the careful arrangement of her body that she had taken to hold herself on the roof was broken. She was slipping and going down fast. Screaming wasn't going to help. There wasn't anyone for miles to hear it. But before she hit the ground, her sound could be heard the length of the wind.

The road stretched for miles before him. Even at night he could see into forever. Dotted with millions and millions of lights, the dark sky was breathtaking. Years before he remembered that he had brought a telescope home one evening and the two of them had spent the night attempting to bring God's creations closer to them. Dakota barked at the wind that passed his face and brought Wheeler back to the moment.

"Thanks boy. You knew what I was thinking. Old fools try their best to recall the finest moments of their past and don't stay focused on what lies before them. I think you just saved me again."

As they rounded the curve in the road, Wheeler felt as though they had entered another dimension. The road seemed to lift from the earth, intimidating him in ways he'd always thought impossible. Try as he might he couldn't turn Stanley's steering wheel. Nor would the brakes work. Moving at a speed much faster than he thought possible, he looked down at Dakota who had pulled his head in from the outside of Stanley and had buried it, both paws over his eyes, deep into the crevice of the old cloth front seat. Motionless and silent sat a fearful Dakota. Upright and panicked sat Sam Wheeler who no longer had the voice to respond to his own question of "what in the world's going on?" Suddenly they were really airborne, no road beneath them other than the filtered invasions of the wind as it drifted by.

Chapter Three

When July awoke she was on a bed in a cabin not too dissimilar from the house she lived in. Trying to sit up and focus she momentarily felt the room spin. Giving into it, her head hit her pillow hard. She closed her eyes and tried to think and then slowly reopened them. Afraid to attempt another sit up, she just laid there, moving her eyes in a circular motion as she allowed them to trace the perimeter of the room. She took in the familiar, even if it was not of the moment. Slowly she turned on her side and raised her head, this time with complete upper body movement as her senses took in the odds and ends scattered around her bed.

Jeff Gutterman

"My God. What's going on here?" her eyes falling on a picture of herself and Wheeler on Wildfire, Wheeler's old thoroughbred.

"I put that picture away years ago," astonishment on her face as she also took in another and yet another framed photo of the two of them scattered around the room. But it wasn't to end there. The more she scanned the room the more she noticed a variety of items that were hers, that had been theirs, that were no longer a part of her present life. An angel that Wheeler had bought her for her birthday years ago; an oversized teddy bear that he had won for her at the County Fair over in Carbon County after knocking down four tin solders in one throw of a softball; a large distorted vase that the two of them had formed from wet clay, baked and painted with an array of cryptic symbols over its sides; and on the bedside a small golden ring that he had given to her several months before they had said their good-byes.

She started to cry. Confusion and the force of her memories left little to be still for. All around her was her past. A past she longed to have in her now. When her eyes cleared, her gaze fell on a small notebook that also held the air of a memory. She reached for it, moving it close to her heart before opening the cover. When she did, the tears again began to fall. Written on the corner of the first page was some scribbling she knew immediately. Out loud she read, "A moment is forever if you hold it in your heart long enough. There will always be people in our life that come and go. Every once in a while one of these people becomes very special to us and we want them with us always. You're that special person to me. Although the seasons change with each gentle wind that blows, my thoughts of you will never diminish. Now and Forever." It was signed Wheeler and before it began was the name July.

Wheeler felt something heavy and warm covering his body. When he opened his eyes he found himself staring up into two small dark globes. Startled at first, his eyes opened about as wide as they could get. Then he saw the teeth and knew he could relax. It was Dakota, stretched over his stomach as though protecting him from the unknown.

"God I've got to stop feeding you. Will you get off of me."

With a sloppy lick of Wheeler's face, Dakota forced himself up but refused to move from over him.

"I think I broke my back which means I can't lift you off of me, so you've gotta move on your own . . . please."

Not a budge.

What Wheeler couldn't immediately see because his focus was on Dakota, was the mist that surrounded the two of them. A thick white fog like nothing he had experienced before. It only became apparent when Dakota decided to remove himself from over Wheeler and sit down beside him, allowing him to concentrate on what else had happened and see around himself a little better. His expression said it all, and he now knew why Dakota was acting protective, unwilling to remove himself from his side.

"Dakota, I appreciate it, but I don't need protecting, and you've got nothing to be frightened of. Move over a little."

When Wheeler stood he was slanted a little to his left, not so much with a broken back but not completely unaffected. As he turned his head looking for Stanley, he once again noticed the dense white fog, and was barely able to make out the trees in its grasp through its water particles. By the time he did notice the first tree it was too late. Head first into it he had bounced off like a rubber ball, once again finding himself on the ground beside Dakota.

July

With tears forming in his eyes from his sudden impact with nature, he began to sit up. "Ouch," was all he said as his hand traced a soft spot on his head. Trying to stand, his legs felt rubbery and he went back down real quick. His second try was better. As he looked around, not wanting to make a move until he was a little more confident of the terrain, he noticed that Dakota was missing.

"That's strange. He was here just a minute ago. Hey boy, where are you? This is no time to play games. Dakota!"

A stifled bark from the interior of the mist pushed a reluctant Wheeler forward. "Keep barking boy. I'm walking toward you as fast as I can, which I'll be the first to admit, isn't too fast."

Following the sound of Dakota's bark for what seemed like an eternity, he was finally able to find him. But not before he tripped over him. "Ahhhh."

Now on his stomach and groaning, he began to lift his head and view the landscape before him. To say the least, he was startled. He knew the cabin, but didn't understand. Jerking his head from one side to the other, trying to both clear his thoughts and take in every inch of space possible, he finally refocused on the cabin.

"I've got to be hallucinating. What do you think of that Dakota? Do you see it, or is it only me?"

Dakota didn't waste a second. With an energy that made Wheeler shiver on the inside, he ran through the rest of the mist toward the cabin as fast as he could. Slowly Wheeler followed him. With each step it seemed a lifetime was passing within him. And for the first time in all the years he could remember, he felt frightened. Much more so than when Stanley had lifted into the air.

From the outside you could see light through the windows. But what was most unsettling was an outline of a person with long hair, moving through its space, marking one window and then the next, as though they were pacing back and forth. About fifteen feet from the door was a tree that Wheeler remembered planting many years ago. He thought it was positioned differently than the picture in his mind, but nonetheless slowly moved toward it at lightning speed. His hands began to trace its trunk about midway up its height. Nothing. He knew the initials they had carved should be there but there was nothing. His eyes searched everywhere. Still nothing.

"I don't believe this," frantic now as he stepped back to appraise both the cabin and the tree and the shadow inside that had paralyzed his heart moments before. His eyes focused on the apparition beyond the windows that extended a lifetime of warm memories.

"I don't understand Dakota. It is but it isn't. What's going on here?"

Dakota had already started for the rear of the cabin. Wheeler took his lead and followed. He stopped abruptly before he came to the turn that would allow him a visual of yesterday. Dropping his head momentarily with eyes closed, one foot trailed by the other, he slowly began making passage beyond the turn. And then he saw him.

"My God. Wildfire? Wildfire, is that you boy?"

Dakota barked and Wildfire neighed, each reaching and bending to touch the other. When Wheeler had reached them he put his hands on Wildfire, a softness in his heart causing him to mount him and stroke his head. "You're not supposed to be here boy. I lost you years ago to a fall."

A soft melodic voice, carried on the water particles of the mist, cut Wheeler's thoughts, total suspension of where he was or that he was on top of Wildfire. "Is there someone out here?" was all it said, before he hit the ground and made his way toward the familiar voice.

Chapter Four

If energy could talk it would tell you that it's around us at all times. A stone, a plant, an animal and ourselves as physical human beings, are all made up of its invisible strands of thought. We move through it from space to space, backward and forward, leaving our vibrational specks of light in every imaginative consideration. Wheeler and July had always remained connected, even when they were apart. Geography didn't matter. Nor did time. The thought of each other had always kept them together.

The knock on the door was loud. From inside July thought someone was breaking it down. At first it frightened her, but her composure came fast. As she made her way to the door she felt her heart begin to quicken. When she opened it she thought it was going to fly from her chest.

Wheeler's mouth was half open, his eyes immovable melons. They stood and stared at each other, each trembling, neither giving into movement or voice. The seasons changed before the silence was broken by Dakota.

"It's okay boy, it's really her."

"Dakota!" was as much as July's weak voice could muster.

Wheeler felt weak, seemed to lose his balance and grabbed a post to steady himself. July immediately went to his side. He was the first to speak. "I've been looking for you everywhere. I don't understand how I've found you. . . . I . . . don't . . ."

July put her arms around his neck, raised her head to gaze into his eyes, and pressed her lips to his, touching the edge of his mouth with a softness of breath he'd never forgotten. For a moment neither existed. They floated on a feathered cloud, far beyond their physical senses.

"I love you, Wheeler. I don't know how you came to be here, but I never want you to leave."

"I'm not going anywhere. For the rest of my life I'm not going anywhere."

July

He brought her toward him again and squeezed hard enough he thought to remove the life force from her. He wanted so badly to meld her essence into his so they'd never be separated again. And she returned the feelings. Neither wanted to talk or move, just to hold on, let the world fall away behind them and life would still be wonderful and exciting.

With their arms around each other they slowly made their way into the small cabin. Wheeler was the first to stop, his eyes taking in the surroundings.

"It's just as I remembered it. Nothing's changed. Nothing!"

"I know . . ."

"This isn't possible but it's happening."

"The last thing I remember was flying through the air in Stanley. Nothing beneath us, just space. Dakota was hanging out the window howling at God only knows what, and I was sitting there wetting my pants."

Her laugh made him smile. It was the gentle melodic voice he had kept in his head for years. He stepped back for a moment and took her in, smiling with wonder at every wonderful wrinkle that outlined her smile.

"All I remember was falling from my roof. I remember screaming on my way down but not actually hitting the ground. But you know what I do remember? A few moments before falling I was playing with a few of our old friends."

"Old friends?"

"Hamlet and Sunshine."

Wheeler's brow furrowed only for a second before his eyes widened and he said, "The doves?"

"The doves!"

Wheeler's hand went instinctively to his forehead. "Say, tell me something? Are we around water of some kind? I've never seen mist like the mist that covers this area and I've never ever seen it in Montana."

"Montana. What makes you think you're in Montana? That's over two thousand miles from here."

"Two thousand miles from here? You can't be right. I was just starting to cross the State line when Stanley took to the air. Just where do you think we are?"

"Texas. Just outside of Beaumont by the Louisiana border."

"Not possible!"

Before she could think the words flew from her mouth, "Wheeler, I know where I live."

"You said you fell off of your roof. How do you explain being in a cabin that we both know is a long way from any part of Texas?"

Now it was July's turn to allow momentary confusion in as she raised her hand to cover her mouth. Without letting go of Wheeler she moved her head back ever so slightly and for the second time since her arrival, began to scan the room. In a breath she filled her lungs with all she could get, seemingly fighting for air, for oxygen, and took in what she had no explanation for. Then she started to laugh. "This is all pretty strange, isn't it? I mean, I was on my roof a long way from where we are now . . . Wheeler, I've never wanted to see or be with anyone more than you. Your image, your essence, has been in my every thought for months . . ."

"Me too. But It's not in me to believe that we've created this through just desire. There's something else at work here." He closed his eyes and pulled her into him so tightly they became one. And then opened them and just smiled. "Is that a glass of wine I see over there?"

"It's Cordaria. Our favorite. I found it in the refrigerator."

Parting, but not letting go, they moved toward the bed where July had found herself when she first awoke. On the bedside stand next to it she picked up the bottle to pour him a glass. And then she laughed. "I don't want to let go either, but I can't open and pour with only one hand."

"You hold the bottle, I'll open." She did and he did, pouring Wheeler a glass. He lifted the glass to his face to take in the aroma.

"Yep, our favorite."

There was a long silence before Wheeler spoke again. When he did, July couldn't. Tears formed in her eyes and trickled down the sides of her cheeks. He had let go of her hand and stepped back. She knew what he was going to ask.

"Why did you ever leave? I thought everything was so good between us. One day you're there, the next you're not. You broke my heart. You hurt me, you hurt us."

"I broke my own heart. I never wanted to leave. I just didn't think you loved me enough." Bowing her head the next words from July came with great pain. "Do you know you never said you loved me."

"Never said I loved you? I said it in everything I did. In every action I took."

"But you never came right out and said it."

Now Wheeler began to tear. "I know."

"Wheeler, you hurt me. Just the fact that you couldn't tell me what you were feeling made me feel that it wasn't going to last. I know you showed me that you cared. That's what's stayed with me these years. But God it's nice to hear the words."

"It's a very hurtful regret. You were a good teacher. I've learned."

July had a sigh of resignation in her expression. "Have you?"

"Where did you go to? I looked all over for you. When I couldn't find you in town I went into anything that resembled a town within a couple hundred miles. I looked and looked, showed your picture to a thousand people. Nothing."

"Wheeler?"

July's eyes were locked onto Wheeler's, his onto hers. Once again July thought they were mind dancing. She started to tear but for a moment only.

"Damn it Wheeler. You still can't say it."

Dakota began to bark from outside, but it didn't seem to phase either one of them. Wheeler grabbed July's arms which had begun hitting his chest. With a secure grip he pulled her to him and smiled.

"In my fifty years I've never loved anyone more. You gave me my first breath when we met. When you left I just dried up inside. And when I couldn't find you I didn't care to go on. For a long time now the walls of my heart have felt like very thin paper that would break apart at the slightest tug. The mental games I've played with myself haven't helped. I can only describe what I felt when I lost you by asking you to picture something like the weight of a couple hundred elephants, trying to dance on a very delicate mental table glass. You need to know. I want you to know. That with all my heart I love you, and nothing and I mean nothing, means as much to me as the two of us together."

"This is a second chance for us. Most people don't get a first. I don't know why and I certainly don't know how, but we're going to make the best of it. We're going to use this time together to be together as two people deeply in love should be."

Dakota's barking had turned to intermittent howling and that caught the attention of both of them. Together they re-traced their steps to the door. But as Wheeler reached for it he stopped short, a question in his eyes that was unmistakable. Without looking at him July caught the concern in his eyes and the hesitation in his movement and was the first to speak his thought.

"Maybe we shouldn't open it. Whatever is going on out there is out there. It's not in here."

He turned to face her but there was nothing to say. She put her hand on his forearm and together they reached for the doorknob. As they touched it there was a tingling sensation that threaded its way through both of them, getting stronger and stronger as the knob was turned enough to clear the door latch and the door was pulled open. What their field of vision allowed was seen all around the area of the small cabin, winding, twisting and floating its way toward them. They held tighter to each other than either of their memories had allowed.

Chapter Five

July found herself stretched out on the ground between a pile of freshly raked leaves on one side, and the hammer that had fallen with her on the other. Positioned as though she had been attempting jumping jacks in midair, her arms were outstretched beyond her head with her legs spread wide apart. She tried to move and found it painful.

"God, what happened?"

Her eyes searched the sky above and slowly her memory came into focus. She'd fallen from the roof. But wait a minute. There was something more. She tried to think, to center her thoughts. The last thing she remembered was . . . the doves.

The doves flying away into the light. There was something else. Something important. Something very important. She raised her head and tried to move again. The pain was still there but with effort she made it to a sitting position.

And then she had it. "My God. Wheeler. W-h-e-e-l-e-r! W-h-e-e-l-e-r! Where are you?"

July frantically searched the grounds with her eyes. Nothing but the weeds and the wind. Nothing. She tried to get up, at first to no avail. On the second try she performed better, raising herself from the sitting position to her full height. A gust of wind commanded her long hair and with an invisible hand blew it into her face, momentarily blinding her from seeing anything. With the brush of a forehand she moved it behind her and began to walk around the grounds of the house.

Her shouts were panicked and filled with an element of fear. In a soft voice first and then a somewhat agitated, much louder sound. "W-h-e-e-l-e-r! W-h-e-e-l-e-r! Please. Don't be gone."

In the distance, a light funnel of dust could be seen and in seconds a truck moved into view from its interior. It was headed toward the house and July. Winding and weaving over the bumps in the dirt road it finally found its resting place about fifty feet from where July was now kneeling, beside a tree in the front yard.

Removing himself from the truck and heading in her direction, he couldn't see her face as he approached, but he could hear her silent tears. When he was within several steps of reaching her he knew all was not well. Bending down to her, he laid a gentle hand on her shoulder. "Something must be terribly wrong. July, it's me, Simple Joe. Has something happened?"

She didn't look up to acknowledge his presence, but her friend's gentle caring voice was met with safety and the tears started flowing uncontrollably. "I don't understand this. I was with Wheeler in the cabin just a moment ago and now I'm not. I think I'm going crazy."

"Wheeler. As in California Wheeler?"

All she could do was shake her head to make him understand.

"That's wonderful. You've mentioned him to me a couple of times before. I had a feeling you wanted to see him again and now he's here."

"No, he's not here."

"But you just said . . . "

"That I was with Wheeler in the cabin."

"What cabin? There's a house here. Not a cabin in sight."

"I know. It doesn't make sense."

Simple Joe just sat down on the ground beside her and scratched his head. "A cabin huh? And Wheeler too?"

July just nodded. "I'm crazy right? Been out here a little too long by myself."

"You're not by yourself kiddo. I come out to see you everyday."

"I know. What would I do without you?"

"Tell me about Wheeler and the cabin."

"What's to tell. I imagined it all. . . . but it was so real. Hamlet and Sunshine. Wildfire and Dakota. All the pictures of us. It was all there . . . Shit! I'm losing it!"

Simple Joe just sat and listened while July related her story. When she finished he just reached up and scratched his head. "Maybe when you fell you hit the ground harder than you think. That can do strange things to us physicals."

"I guess so. There's no other explanation . . . But it was so real."

"You wanted it so much you kinda made it happen for yourself while you were knocked out. It's like thinking about something just before you drop off to sleep and then having a dream about it. You know how that happens."

July just shook her head. "Walk with me?"

"Of course."

Together they headed toward the back of the house and then started on down a well-worn path the two of them had walked many times before. If you were standing behind them you would have occasionally seen Simple Joe's arm reach up over July's shoulders as though confirmation of the safety of his friendship.

July had met Simple Joe the first week she had moved in, and was quite thankful for it. She had pulled up to the house with a small enclosed trailer attached to her car, packed in only the way a woman could pack one. There wasn't an inch of unused space within its covering. Crammed into each dark corner was a piece of July's life. She had made it all fit. Her memories were scattered over miles and miles of landscape but her physical possessions were within the boundaries of the trailer.

She saw him coming from a mile away. When he got out of his truck he just stood, scratched his head, and appraised the trailer. "Well, how long you think it'll take the two of us to unload that thing, assuming of course we don't have to Vaseline everything in there down to get it out?"

She had just laughed. And it was contagious. Before formal introductions had taken place they were both exchanging the musical notes of laughter. It took them both the rest of the day to unload July's belongings. Simple Joe had introduced himself as a local rancher, retired long ago. He had once had a daughter about July's age but a virus had taken her. He missed her a lot but wouldn't talk about that part of it. Not immediately anyway. When she had asked him how he came to be called Simple Joe he just smiled and said he had always chided his friends about how complicated they had made their lives, and how unhappy most of them were. "It just came about I guess." Two of his friends, now passed on, had come up with it at the same time.

Their friendship had grown immensely over time, and July was grateful. Daily visits by Simple Joe, a breakfast here, a lunch there, a dinner every now and then. But always, always, good conversation. July had told Simple Joe that he reminded her of her own father who had died when she was very young. She had adored him and had gone into a deep depression for a long time when he had passed away. Her mother had often said she was inconsolable and for many years was just that. There had always been more friends in July's life than special relationships and maybe because of it she had never married. She had often wondered if losing her father had anything to do with that. Loving someone so much and then not having them around. Never wanting to repeat it. Always keeping a safe distance from deep involvement.

She had told Simple Joe that Wheeler had been the exception. She had opened to him completely and totally. And was devastated when she had to leave. Although the circumstances were a little different, that was something Simple Joe had understood very well. His wife had left him years before in somewhat the same manner. After his daughter had died he said he just dried up inside, didn't want human contact of any kind anymore.

So the friendship blossomed. As much as she had grown to love Simple Joe and what he represented to her, she understood full well that he had his own cuts and scars, his own life bruises, and in understanding would accommodate his occasional sadness as it seeped into their conversations.

Chapter Six

Stanley was moving along just fine when all of a sudden the front of him pitched forward and downward as the brake pads made their way into the steel rotor that was a part of his braking system. Wheeler looked scared to death.

"What the hell is going on here?"

When Wheeler had slammed on the brakes, Dakota had answered with a howl, sliding from his seat next to his master on down to the floor.

"Dakota, I think I'm going nuts."

He got out of the jeep, slammed the door and just looked around. "I don't believe this. Two minutes ago I was standing in my old cabin with my arm around July and now I'm God knows where. What in the world is going on here."

Behind him a pair of small, golf ball size globes, growing in size with each passing moment, made their way closer to them. Every now and then they seemed to disappear for a second or so and then reappear as though they had always been there. It was as black as the night sky, the moon not really choosing to perform tonight, the old highway lit only by Stanley's headlights in front of them and whatever was coming toward them from behind. When the lights disappeared once again behind where Wheeler and Dakota were standing, Wheeler raised his arms from his side, chest height, palms up, as if to say, "Yeah, what now."

It seemed like hours but finally the car was within a stone's throwing distance. Wheeler stood out on the blackened old highway and tried to flag the driver, get them to stop. Dakota, not sure just what to do, began running around him in circles. Ever so slowly the car slowed its pace and approached the two figures with sincere caution. With the headlights hitting them just so, they looked like a circus act gone wrong. Wheeler, waving at the driver, first with one arm and then the other, Dakota making the circuit around Wheeler. The two blonde globes, now definitely defined as headlights, were searching for position as the car coasted to a halt.

"Hey, can you help us?"

The window on the driver's side slid from the top of the door frame and its owner stuck her head beyond its fixed location. "Hi, having some trouble?"

Wheeler noticed that she was very pretty as he approached. "Not trouble exactly, just lost."

"You're on 'old 55' headed north from the looks of your jeep."

"Yeah, that's what I thought. Just needed some verification . . . Whereabouts though, I mean on 'old 55'?"

"Well, you're about forty miles due south of Calabasas County. Does that help?"

Wheeler answered by just sitting down where he had been standing, next to the car in the middle of the street. "Miss, do I look like I'm nuts?"

Her car window started making its way back up toward the top of the door frame, stopping with just enough of an opening left so that she could speak. "Looks can be deceiving. I'd be out of place answering that one."

"A few minutes ago I was four hundred miles from here in the middle of a minor forest. Now I'm here again."

Jeff Gutterman

The car was still running and she had one foot on the brake and the other on the gas so she felt fairly safe. Once again the window began to re-open. "Here again?"

"Yeah, again. I've been driving on this road most of the night. Then all of a sudden I find myself in midair moving through the wind without a road under me. Then I'm in the forest and now I'm back here again."

It didn't take a moment's thought. She smiled, waved, and her foot hit the gas pedal like she was a racer for the Indianapolis 500. After a minute or so she was clean out of sight.

"Com'on Dakota. Let's move Stanley off the road and sack out for a few hours. Don't think anyone else is coming this way this time of night that's going to want to talk to us."

Lightning, loud and long hit their ears before they made it back to Stanley. By the time they got seated they were both drenched.

"Great, all we have to do now is wait for the earthquake."

An hour or so later they were fast asleep, Wheeler snoring at a decibel rate similar to a gas powered engine, but for some reason just below what it would have taken to wake Dakota. Wheeler was gone, sleeping the sleep of a newborn, every now and then tears silently rolling down his checks, a release from the dream that had overtaken him.

It started as all warm dreams do, wrapping you in their energy, making you feel safe. He was back in the area of the cabin but it was years ago, another time, another him. July was behind him holding tight.

"Sweetie, he's stopped running. We can get off now."

He felt her hold tighter and that caused him to turn and kiss her. Ever so slowly they both began dismounting from Wildfire. When they hit the ground their embrace was solid. They drew back from each other several moments later and hand in hand headed for the cabin. All of a sudden July bolted. In a moment it was obvious why.

"No, you wouldn't. July don't do that. Please don't do that."

Too late. The spray was coming full force at him. He tried to move out of range but the hose had over a hundred feet to it and July was extending it running toward him. He was getting wet. Very wet. He tried to run toward her but she was good at dodging his attack. Now he was completely soaked.

"You're gonna be sorry for this."

"Who're you kidding. You're so tired from the ride you're not going to do anything. No strength left."

Or so she thought. He whistled for Wildfire and he obliged. In a moment he was standing on the instrument of Wheeler's destruction and the outgoing water shower was cut off. July was no dummy. She knew exactly when to retreat. And retreat she did. Running and screaming toward the front door of the cabin as Wheeler grabbed the hose and pulled it from under Wildfire's foot releasing a couple hundred pounds of pressure that had been storing itself. She never made it close to the door. The water hit her with such a force that she slipped and landed face down on the ground.

When she recovered the first words out of her mouth were, "that wasn't fair!"

"You're right. I never should have started this." In a moment he was on the ground with her, both of them rolling into each other's arms.

"I love you so much Wheeler. Don't you dare ever leave me. I'd be lost without you."

"You're every thought I think lady. I'm not going anywhere. In fact, I'm so happy with where

I'm at at this moment that I'm not going to allow it to end. It's going to go on forever and ever and then some."

She smiled up at him with one of those sad whimsical smiles, one of surrender, that only a lady deeply in love could generate. The last thing he remembered before the cave were her eyes. Deeply opening, pulling him into her world and then . . .

The cave. Moving this way and that, carrying both of them down an unknown path toward more unknowingness. He remembered how July had initially described the adventure to him, before Dakota had been asked by her to get him. She said she had discovered it the day before with a little help from Dakota, when they were out for their early morning walk. It was back behind the cabin about half a mile, lodged in the side of a hill. The opening was tight, but large enough for her to squeeze through, which she did, but only after Dakota had come out suggesting it was fine to go exploring. And they did. For about a hundred feet, before it became a narrow tunnel, dipping sharply downward. That was when she made the decision she wanted Wheeler's company on this adventure. Dakota had been the messenger. When they both showed up about twenty minutes later Wheeler was out of breath. When he saw her smile he just leaned against the cave wall and openly panted.

"The way Dakota came running into the cabin I thought something had happened to you. I ran most the way."

She kissed him lightly. "Thank you for the thought sweetie, but I'm okay. Look what I found."

"It looks like just some old hole in the dirt."

"Follow me."

She led him through the cave entrance down through its corridor until they reached the narrow walls that resembled more of a tunnel than a cave. Wheeler stopped the same way July had when they reached this part.

"I feel like we're treading on sacred ground."

"You do not. You're just scared to go further."

"Dakota boy. Why don't you run on down that way and see just what's down there."

"I told you. Just scared."

"Don't crock that nose too far in the air. You didn't send Dakota back for me because you felt like Columbus."

"Do you want me to go first?"

"Honey, that's a great idea."

July moved ahead of Wheeler, started out and then stopped.

"Wait a minute. I can run faster than you. You should be going first."

"What are you talking about."

"If there's rough ground down there I'm not going to be able to run out of here. This tunnel's so narrow and you're so slow that all I'll be able to do is keep running into you."

"Cute, real cute. Move on little girl."

It was the strangest passage July had ever seen. It just kept turning and turning and going down and down. What guided them was a haze of light somewhere off in the distance. Just enough illumination to see the shadows of their hands and feet as they touched the walls for guidance. July sensed they walked for an hour. Wheeler would later tell her it was less than five minutes.

The speck of light was growing large as they approached. Momentarily transfixed on where she was, she screamed as Wheeler touched her back with his hand.

"Whoa girl. Just me."

"Sorry. I was wondering how long this thing was and what was at the end of it and for a second there I forgot you were in back of me."

"Uh oh. Already forgetting I'm with you. Not a good sign."

"Quiet, I hear something."

July was right. There was music coming from ahead. Gentle soothing music. And more light. Flickering light. It didn't take long. Another several turns and they entered a small room. Nothing special. A table at its center made of old boxes and crates. It was covered with a tablecloth and a bottle of Cordaria wine sitting in a bucket of ice. There were candles everywhere. Bright flickering candles. Long ones. They were all yellow. That was her favorite color. Taking it all in she caught the sound of the music in a familiar place within her. It was their song. She started to turn around to find Wheeler's eyes but they landed on the tablecloth first and on his note. "Now and Forever. Happy Anniversary." She started to cry . . .

He felt a stab deep in his solar plexus and bent forward in pain. When he opened his eyes he was looking through Stanley's windshield at the cold black rainy night before him.

Chapter Seven

Outside the clouds were a light gray, the sky drawn with tiny lance-like droplets of water. Some of them disappeared in the air currents before hitting the ground while the remaining tear-shaped drops landed independently, dissolving quickly into the earth and surrounding landscape. Sometimes they seemed to come together as they were falling, making a more noticeable showing as they touched their grounded target. It was this kind of a cloud filled lazy afternoon, as he gazed out through Stanley's windshield, that Wheeler noticed his mind once again racing back fifteen years to the time when he had first met her.

Very special at that moment, more so even now. He thought about how memory had a way of expanding that inner vision he was carrying, projecting it to every corner of his mind, recalling his past emotions.

Hazy at first, coming into focus slowly but clearly, was Wheeler on Wildfire. They had just finished a long run and were within a hundred yards of the house. Stopping to let Wildfire snatch some grass from the ground, he sensed a physical form off to his left and turning to look found a lady. Clad in shorts and sneakers she had become captive of a mulberry bush, slowly and with intent, picking what she could of its fruit. He watched for a moment and then cautiously approached.

"Careful. Those can be awfully good if they're ripe."

She heard his voice and had knowingly and slowly turned toward him. A smile from her lips spread across her face, lighting up both of their souls.

"And if they're not ripe?"

"Bitter taste. Very bitter. Everything has its time. You can't push nature."

She picked one and silently reached up and handed it to him. "Let's pretend that I'm the

Queen and you're one of my subjects testing it to see if it's matured."

"Ahh. Psychological captivity. Not my cup of tea. I might lie to you."

"Can't happen. You're expression would give you away."

He nodded, bit into it and his face fell into a fixed contortion. They both laughed. He noticed her hair bounce on her shoulders as she raised her head to met his gaze. She was beautiful. More beautiful than anything he had ever seen or anyone he had ever met. He was smitten. Without saying anything he lowered his arm to help her up on Wildfire. Without a moments hesitation she wrapped her hands around the offering and was helped onto his back. The last thing he remembered was her enchanted scream as Wildfire took to the open spaces. He could feel her behind him, not just in her grasp but in an all encompassing way. At first when her arms encircled him he felt chills race up and down his body. Now he was tingling from head to toe. It just wasn't stopping. He knew she was someone special.

He could feel her dark green eyes piercing his mind and entering his soul, taking control of all his senses. At first it startled him. Then he just relaxed and allowed the feeling. It was warm all over and he was smiling a smile he knew she wouldn't see, sitting behind him as she was.

They raced for ten minutes before he felt something sharp dig into his shoulder. Without knowing why, he knew she had caused it. The choice was his. He could keep going and look or bring them to a stop and look. It took a split second to decide.

"Whoa boy, whoa!

One hand released the rein and reached up to touch the place where he had felt the pain a second before. His fingers landed on a wet shirt through which he could trace the indentations of teeth marks.

"It didn't hurt that much did it?"

"You bit me!"

"Yeah. Couldn't think of another way to get you to stop."

"You bit me!"

"I need to get off. I think I need a pair of jeans to ride. The inside of my thighs are going to be tingling for a week."

She jumped down from Wildfire, wobbly-legged at first and then ran her hands over her inner thighs. He glanced toward her problem knowing he would be a gentleman and look only momentarily, but now unable to pull himself out of a self-induced trance-like state. She reached over and socked his leg and that immediately brought him back to life.

"Ouch! Say, do you do anything but bite and hit?"

"Yes, but first find me a pair of jeans."

"That's easy although I think they'll be a little big on you."

He reached behind where July had been sitting and unfastened the small leather pouch that was in back of the saddle. Reaching in he pulled out a pair of off-white crinkled pants, encircled at the waist by a drawstring, and handed them to her.

"These are the funniest looking jeans I've ever seen."

"That's because they're not jeans. They're what I sleep in when I camp out. But if they're not good enough for you because they're not denim . . ."

She didn't say a word as she slipped into them with ease. Wheeler could feel a smile creep into his mind as he noticed they were way too big for her, but was too much of a gentleman to mention it again.

She thought otherwise though. "Good fit!"

"I think you've got them on backwards."

"What makes you say that?"

"Nothing much. Just that you're going to be sitting on some buttons when you climb back on Wildfire."

"I thought I felt something strange back there. Why'd you wait so long to tell me?"

"I just allow people to do what they do. Everybody's different. Sometimes they make sense and sometimes not. Besides, most of us remember better if we learn from our own mistakes. My guess is that next time you'll put them on with the buttons in the front."

"The next time. Aren't you taking a lot for granted? I don't even know your name."

"Wheeler."

"Just Wheeler?"

"Sam Wheeler. But just Wheeler will do."

"I like the name Sam."

"So do I, but I've become used to Wheeler."

"I like Wheeler too. Wheeler it is then."

For a moment or two there was a gentle silence that filled the air between them. Gaze matching gaze, at first solid eye contact, then an ever so slight movement as they each in turn took in the complete outline of the other's face.

Wheeler was the first to break the peace. "Beula's a beauutiful name."

"Beula? . . . That wouldn't be your way of asking me what my name is, would it?"

"You weren't offering. I felt compelled to initiate an inquiry. Learned a long time ago that you can't close communication down. A bad thing, real bad thing."

He smiled an ear-wide grin and she relented.

"How are you at matching personalities with names."

"If I went strictly on that I would have called you Sunshine."

Now it was her turn to smile. Just a little, but also from ear to ear.

"July."

"It's full of wonderment and magic."

Wheeler reached down and offered his left arm to July who for the second time today accepted and was lifted onto Wildfire. But it wasn't the gait of a horse and its riders he heard as Wildfire moved into the wind, rather the steady sound of a heavy truck horn forcing him from his mental images of the two of them, back onto the road.

Chapter Eight

Simple Joe stepped from his truck onto a cushion of mud, his boots reaching half-way into the earth's softness before he realized what had happened. Too late in fact to relate the incident to July, to stop her from repeating it. She had opened her door a few seconds after Simple Joe and found her own soft ground.

"Yuk."

"It's only on your boots kiddo. A little water and it's off."

"What boots. I have tennis shoes on!"

"Oh, . . . sorry."

July looked down at her legs and saw the mud half-way to her knees, the tennis shoes having disappeared instantly at ground contact. She just smiled and shook her head.

"Well, as long as we're in this stuff we may as well continue. It's just up the incline over there."

Pointing, Simple Joe forced July to look. Off in the distance she could see a grove of what appeared to be pine trees, thick enough so that they blanketed the side of the hill Joe was pointing to. She made an agreeable smile in his direction, closed her door and started toward the area. Once she reached the incline she had to side step up its steepness for a short distance because of the sloppiness and slipperiness of the ground. Just a couple feet ahead of Joe, she reached the first layer of trees before him. Her concentration was so great that the flash of a small squirrel darting across her path startled her and down she went with a thud-like splash. Simple Joe just stopped and stared, an emotional combination of wanting to laugh and serious consideration, wondering if she had hurt herself.

"Oh no! Joe, will you just look at me."

"Actually you look pretty cute."

The phrase unnerved her and all of a sudden she was staring at Joe without seeing him, actually looking right through him.

"July, you okay? July?"

Nothing. Just this blanket-like expression of being somewhere else. It took only a moment but Simple Joe knew. She was with Wheeler again.

They'd been in the mountains for three days. Lost. Thankfully they had all that was necessary with regard to camping gear. And they weren't actually lost. As cold and wet as it was they were warmed by the presence of each other.

Dakota was with them, at times darting a couple of hundred feet in front of them playing scout, and then returning to walk for a ways by their side.

At one point Wheeler had thrown an old branch he had found lying on the ground for Dakota's pleasure. Even before it had landed Dakota was on his way to it. But he didn't return. Instead he just barked and barked at what appeared to be the old branch. Odd, they both thought as they approached where the branch had landed. Visually neither could see anything out of the ordinary. Then July stepped toward it. Nestled several feet behind the branch and a few feet up from it on their own limb, her eyes gazed on what appeared to be a rainbow of butterflies.

Ten, fifteen, twenty. All different shapes, sizes and colors.

"Wheeler, look at this. Dakota boy, it's okay. Their just some new friends."

"I wonder where they came from. This is the wrong time of year for them. And the wrong temperature."

"They're beautiful. And they don't seem to be afraid of us. They're not flying off."

"So far. I wouldn't get much closer though. That might be pushing it a bit."

She paid no attention to him. Moving slowly she reached out with her hand and placed it just below the tiny branch they were resting on. Two of the brightest most beautiful butterflies she had ever seen made their way from the limb to her arm.

"Wheeler."

"Well, I'll be."

"Try it!"

"You have a gentler soul than I do and I think they'll sense it and fly away. I may ruin it for you."

"Nonsense. Stick your hand over by them."

Slowly and cautiously Wheeler responded. So did the butterflies. Several more moved from the limb they were on to Wheeler's sleeve.

"See. Your soul is just as gentle as mine."

It was then that they heard it. A cooing kind of sound. They passed a glance back and forth and then all around themselves but couldn't find it.

"Dakota! Where's the sound coming from?"

Dakota just laid down on the moist ground and looked at the two of them.

"Big help."

"Wheeler, look!"

Wheeler raised his head to where July was pointing. Circling above them were two white doves. When they knew they had been spotted they landed next to the butterflies, each keeping physical contact with the other.

"July, I think they're doves. Awful friendly ones."

"I think the small one is the male."

"You would think that."

"No really, look. Isn't it usually the male that shows off. Look what he's doing. His neck is moving up and down and he's moving it over her back."

"You might be right. The other one is just sitting there relaxing while the male does all the work."

"Look how bright she looks. Let's name them."

"How about Anthony and Cleopatra!"

"How about Hamlet and Sunshine?"

"It fits. Done."

By this time several butterflies had landed on Dakota but he paid little attention to them. He was watching and approving of the interplay of Wheeler and July with the doves. When Wheeler turned to him he noticed that his gaze was fixed on July and that caused him to also turn his full attention to her.

"Yes, I'd say so."

"You'd say so what?"

"That actually you look pretty cute. You, the butterflies and the doves."

"July! July! Old friend to July, are you there?"

He had broken the trance. July looked up and focused onto the smiling eyes of Simple Joe. Involuntarily she returned his smile, but then the immediate memory of Wheeler turned her wistful grin into a far more melancholy expression.

Chapter Nine

They were back at her house, Simple Joe in the kitchen creating what he called his magic. And in the pot on the stove was indeed a magical brew. Chopped carrots and a sprinkling of fennel coated with the smallest peas anyone had ever seen. Laced with both yellow and orange peppers, a drop of Jamaican Rum, and a scoop of a striped herb that had a bluish tint to it. This was the only thing in the pot that Joe wouldn't identify.

"It'll put hair on your chest."

"I don't want hair on my chest."

"Too late, it's already in the mix."

"What would I do without you? You always seem to be here when I need a shoulder to cry on."

"Isn't that what friendship's all about?"

She just smiled that ever widening smile of hers. He offered his in return.

"I'm going to step outside in the air for a moment."

"Enjoy yourself. I've got ten more minutes of stirring and simmering to go. I'll call you."

Taking off her shoes she headed toward the front door. She couldn't remember opening it though, before finding herself in a familiar garden. In front of her were a couple hundred yards of herbs scattered about and planted in the ground. Some leaned this way, others that. She stopped, glanced around and began to smile. Then she started to run. On the other side of the field of herbs was a small house. The closer she came the easier it was to read the sign, "The Herb Garden Restaurant."

Rounding the corner to the back of the house she reached for the door and almost pulled it off its hinges. Stepping inside she spotted him behind the old wooden chopping board working tirelessly on some vegetables, chopping first and then removing the bits and pieces to a pot simmering on the stove. She was sure her heart jumped several beats and her breathing stopped altogether. It was Wheeler.

"Are you making that for me?"

The upper portion of his body turned and looked toward the voice he knew so well, causing him to generate his own broad smile.

"It's for us. And I've put enough liquor in it to help still all our cares. Would you like a taste?"

"Of course."

He turned completely, a spoon full of juice pushing out from his hand toward her. She started to reach toward it, changed her mind and threw her arms around him causing the contents of the spoon to fly into the air. July found herself squeezing tighter than ever before. He dropped the spoon and returned her hug, lifting her and turning the two of them around in a circle several times before depositing her once again to the ground. They exchanged glances but not a sound.

July was the first to speak. "How did you know I'd be here?"

Wheeler just shook his head and smiled. "There's magic in the air. I don't claim to understand it, but I accept it. It's given me back what I've wanted for a long time now and I've stopped looking gift horses in the mouth. When I found myself walking through an herb field with a warmed sky from out of our past, miles from any other living creature, when just a second before that Dakota and I were sitting in Stanley looking out at melting raindrops, well . . . there's wizardry and enchantment in the air. There are magicians up there playing with their puppets and their hearts. I think they're giving us the chance to open some old wounds, look at how they came about, and close them if we can."

"And if we can?"

"Maybe we can stay together."

"And if we can't."

"Then we may be caught in a never ending circle of emotion we'll never be able to control. And we'll probably continue to float from one reality to the next, waiting with all our hearts for a chance to come together again just one more time."

July stepped back from Wheeler and tilted her head a little to one side. She glanced first at the floor and then directly into his eyes. "That doesn't sound very enjoyable. I mean floating forever, always reaching for the gold you can never quite grasp."

"I agree. Seems there's only one solution. Come here."

He needn't of asked. She was in his arms again, squeezing with all her might, never wanting to let go. Slowly, ever so slowly, continuing to hold tight, they each moved in unison, moving the upper part of their bodies away from each other just enough to momentarily take in more of the other. Then they kissed, and for the two of them time stood still. They weren't here, they weren't there. They just were. Together.

Wheeler felt chills move up and down his spine, felt his legs become rubbery and for a moment thought he might collapse on the floor. This was ecstasy, more than anything he could have hoped for. July's sense was of light-headedness, a sensation of too much energy leaving her body at one time, taking all conscious thoughts with it. If God had asked them to release each other at that moment or suffer the consequences they both would have accepted their fate as salt.

Neither was aware of themselves or the other. They were one being, male and female caught in the essence of love. Their individual thoughts moved in a pattern of oneness, each melding into the other equally. Neither could move forward nor back. They stayed simply locked within the unity of their spirit.

Wheeler was the first to move, reaching with one arm behind him to turn off the stove. With the other he took July's hand and led her down the narrow wooden hallway to a room that contained only a window and bed. They both tried moving slowly but the future was beginning to race toward them with additional thoughts and emotions. Within seconds they were side by side, July moving over every inch of Wheeler, forcing remembrance of things past. The emotion was too much, Wheeler needed movement, and in seconds his passivity gave way to returning July's offering. Their hearts beating in rhythm, faster and faster as lifetimes past and all the hurt was put to rest, over and over again, binding themselves together in their uninhibited lovemaking.

Nothing had to occur, for they were the occurrence. Nothing had to release or complete itself. They couldn't remember the beginning and there was going to be no end. They had fallen into each other willingly without sight or thought of their surroundings. And with each singular touch the other responded involuntarily, returning the exploration to a new level. Hours passed, the composite on the stove lay exposed, the sun set, and they slept like children.

Chapter Ten

It was the filtered rays of a soft sunrise moving through the slats of the wooden window that began to quietly awaken them. July was the first to stir, her body laced tightly within Wheeler's. Naked and stretched to his full length he lay spent, body akimbo. July lay on her stomach, her right leg draped over a matching leg of Wheelers. It looked as though one of her arms had disappeared beneath her but the other had marked its territory across his chest, her right hand gently touching the side of his face. With eyes still closed she silently began to move. At lightning speed an awakening thought of disappearances past began forming that he might not be there. Fear raced from one corner of her body to the other, causing her to involuntarily kick, moving her overlapping leg in an upward motion toward Wheeler's particulars. Now they were both awake.

"Ahhh!"

July quickly opened her eyes. "Oh thank God, you're still here."

Wheeler did what he could to turn on his side, trying his best to pull his legs up to him. His moans were almost silent, his speech a whisper.

"Ohhh, wasn't there a better way of finding out?"

July shot him a pouting, "I'm sorry" look, that in seconds worked its magic.

When his inner vision of stars began to fade, he gracefully acknowledged her sympathy by nodding his head. A moment later a smirk crossed his lips and he pointed toward the window. "Will you look at that."

What Wheeler was commenting on was the form that had partially entered the bedroom through the window they had left open throughout the night. They both sat up in the bed and stared over at Wildfire who was standing just outside the room but who had silently moved his head in through the opening.

"Kind of a cute picture, don't you think."

"I don't want to ask and I'm not so sure I want to know. But this garden's a long way's from where he was a few hours ago at the cabin."

"But so are we. And a few hours has somehow turned into a far longer span of time than either of us wants to admit."

He smiled "You're right. The magic continues. It's all around us."

"Do you think he wants to take us somewhere?"

"Possibility. But my guess is he wants to see how us humans do it. Besides, right now I'd rather stay right where we are."

For a moment Wheeler thought he'd turned translucent. July's stare was making him feel as though she could see through him, an apparent focus on something far beyond his physical presence. He shook the uncomfortable feeling from deep within and said it again. "I'd rather stay right where we are!"

July seemed to free herself from her vision. "Sweetie, do you love me?"

"More than ever. You know that."

"I want you to do something for me."

"I'd move mountains for you . . . Probably wouldn't get very far, but I'd sure attempt it."

"I want to have a serious talk."

"Can we make love again first?"

Jeff Gutterman

They both looked toward Wildfire and then back at each other.

"He's only a horse. But if it's important to you I could probably talk to him and get him to look the other way."

"I think Wildfire would like Darby."

"Darby?"

"I bought a mare sometime ago. She's beautiful Wheeler. Just a little bit smaller than Wildfire and almost the same color."

July started to laugh and Wheeler, not really comprehending but remembering the contagion of July's moods, started to laugh along with her.

"Do you think he's as confused as we are. I mean about being here one minute and there the next?"

"So that's it, huh? Well, I don't know. I remember reading somewhere that animals don't bind themselves to time the way we do. They just seem to float in the present moment. The rise or setting of the sun doesn't seem to affect them emotionally the way it does us. You know, when the sun's up we play and when it begins to set we've trained ourselves to think in terms of rest and sleep and the ending of another day. They don't do that. Maybe it's the same for them with place? Hard question. Probably an easy answer. You said you wanted to talk?"

"I'm trying to understand how you could let us go the way you did?"

Wheeler drew back just enough to startle even himself. Solemn and apprehensive, feeling like this was a test to see if he could walk across the crate of eggs without breaking any, he approached her question. "This has to be woman's logic, right? Sweetie, I wasn't the one to leave, you were."

"But I wouldn't have left if I'd understood you better. I mean, I feel you're a part of me yet I don't understand how you work inside. Simple words like I love you for someone you love. Why was it so hard? I guess I feel that somehow it ties in with respect for me. If you love someone you tell them. Simple, nothing complicated."

His sigh was heard by Wildfire. He didn't know where to go, how to answer. Nor did he understand why they were covering the same subject again. And in the pit of his stomach there was a knowing creeping up on him that said this issue wasn't ever going to be settled, no matter what he did or how hard he tried. He was at a loss for words.

"Honey, what do I say? I'm sorry for both of us that I didn't get it out the way it should have come out, at the time it should have come out. But

I am convinced that this is a second chance for us both. Can we leave the mistakes in the past?"

"Yes. But I need to really understand you. Now more than ever. And I don't want to wait a lifetime, guessing at all the reasons for why things happen the way they do."

Wheeler took a deep breath and let out another sigh. He looked at July with compassion and understanding, nodded his head and attempted to put to bed once and for all what was such a mystery to her.

"I don't know if I'm going in the right direction with this but I'll try. They say that when you close up a little, and I guess that's what we're talking about here, well, that the reasons for it go back to childhood or thereabouts. I can't trace anything back that far but I can go back somewhere in my early twenties. And please keep in mind while I'm saying this that I don't know if I'm even on course . . ."

Wheeler had July's full attention. She was now sitting on the bed with her legs crossed, her axis point remaining locked on every new angle his face took. While he talked she visually traced every line in his well creased cheeks and forehead, noticed how, when he said certain words and allowed himself to get caught in the emotion they brought, the lower corner of both eyes would emit the smallest amount of liquid, his eyelids blinking just in time to catch and hold back an onslaught of tears. She also noticed how when he squinted his eyes, his brow wrinkled and he became more serious. July knew beyond a shadow of a doubt that Wheeler was speaking from the heart.

" . . .The different love affairs I had in my early years, the ones I thought mattered back then, all became disappointments in one way or another. I gave so much of myself for so little in return. When you put yourself out like that, totally and completely, and it doesn't work the way you want it to, well, it just closes you up so you give less the next time. And each time that happens you remember the hurt and what you may have said that didn't work. Experience was a harsh teacher. The thought of repeating something that caused me so much pain and made me look at myself as having failed became a non-option . . ."

He stopped for a moment and was silent. July moved her head to a resting position in Wheeler's lap, her hand on his leg, his hand on her head, stroking her hair. She had been absorbing all of Wheeler's comments and was now beginning to feel she understood, at least a little. That would be okay for now. She lifted herself and turned to kiss him. He returned the motion but wouldn't prolong it.

"I've got more to say. It's got to come out."

July understood and laid back down, all the while maintaining contact with Wheeler's body, her own hand moving over his legs while he talked.

"I don't see it as being about respect as you had said, but more about choice. I really believe that each action we take in some way is influenced by our past. There are little invisible sign posts that a part of us sees before we take any action. They're like stoplights except they aren't lights at all but words. One of them says 'move forward quickly.' Another says 'move forward but be careful, there are obstacles on this course.' And the other one says 'don't even think about it. Move this way and hurt's right around the corner.' I don't know if I believe in all this talk of reincarnation and other past lives, but I think I understand one thing very clearly. If we do go around again and again, then the memories have to be blocked from us of each previous cycle. Controlling and moving through the memories of just one lifetime can provide enough hurt on their own to stop someone dead in their tracks from ever taking another step in any direction. Harsh memories can stop you from living in the now.

July, honey, I'm sorry if a part of my past caused me not to act and caused you so much pain."

Chapter Eleven

Wheeler and July spent the next several hours in quiet conversation, each touching the heart of the other as they talked of Wheeler's past, and how what he had or hadn't said or done when they were together was affected by it. He had painted his canvas informally as he retraced the various black and white expressions that had moved him in the direction of who he was to become. Unwittingly, he had deeply moved July with stories and comments about his past. And July continued to both amaze and endear herself to Wheeler even more than she already had, by granting recognition to his feelings and the understanding and structure they had brought him in dealing with his life situations. With each nod of the head, each empathetic acknowledgment of what her own personal trials and lessons had been over the years, they grew closer in understanding of the other. But old hurts die hard, even with new understandings, and at times as he spoke, he'd notice her forehead crinkle and a line of confusion form behind the crease. Gliding thoughts that sometimes, the more he confided in her, the more confused she became, grasping incompletely how little she really knew about him.

Wheeler caught the tilt of July's head, her eyes moving to the corner of her mind. "You look a little confused."

"I guess I am. I just always thought that when you fall for someone, when you love them, that you instinctively know everything about them. Their life's trials and sufferings. Their rides to the crest of the mountain and beyond. Their invisible pleasures and hidden pains. I guess I just felt without thinking much about it that you know all these things about the other half of you because of the chemistry that flows between you. But maybe not. I guess that's silly. Maybe all connectiveness is an illusion. All togetherness arbitrary."

"Honey, I don't think you're the only person to labor under an incomplete image of who the other is. We all do it. There's no way we can know everything about each other when we choose to come together at some point. And even if we started out together our conscious thoughts wouldn't necessarily be tuned to the same idea, nor would our inclination to see it the same way be apparent. And that's not even taking into account the possibility of other lives with other people and other places at other times. In a way, we're new to each other each time we meet."

"You talked to me of the times you tried to help people and got pushed away. About how those memories affected us by just what you were willing to say and share with me. I think back at some of the things you said with regard to other people, and in a way it's like I was there. It helps me to better understand some of what went on between us. I can feel your hurt at being rejected when you've put yourself out like that. Why do people feel so defensive when help is offered. Why did I? I don't understand it."

"I didn't understand it at first either. And I'm not so sure that I'm any further along in my consideration of it now. But through the pain has come an education. Part of the lesson was in learning to back off. And maybe that meant not completing verbal thoughts, however beautiful they might have been. Simply to just allow others to move in the direction they choose. It's their choice. Unless they actually ask you for help you're interfering in their decision making process. You've got no right. I had no right."

"You said something to me once a long, long time ago I didn't quite understand, but yet it's always stayed with me. You said we each walk alone by choice, entering and leaving stage plays we create for our own benefit. I'm still not sure I grasp all of it but I think I'm starting to understand a part of what you meant."

"Good. That means we can eat something now." Wheeler smiled and got up, moving to the doorway of the bedroom. With the thickest German accent he could muster he began shouting toward an imaginary maid in the kitchen. "Hilda, it's Frans down in the basement. I've finally found a hostage to all my stories and philosophies. And I'm actually getting her to believe them. If you hear screams coming from here you must ignore them. She'll only be pretending she can't take it anymore and wants out. But remember they're illusionary screams and hold no value whatsoever. By the way, could you fix us up some food good enough for morning munching. We've had a passionate night and an intellectual morning. We're famished!"

July was on the bed smiling up at him, mind blank, living in the moment. She felt she could never love anyone more. He returned to the bed, reached for her face and held it firmly, kissing her softly on the forehead. Moving only his head back, he took her in for the hundredth time, and then placed his lips on her mouth and kissed her with a gentleness greater then he had ever achieved in the past.

"I want to tell you a story that I think will sum up what I've been trying to say."

"What will Hilda think when she comes with our food?"

"She's already heard this so she'll be perfectly fine with hearing it again."

"Figures."

Wheeler grabbed a couple of pillows, pounded soft spots into each and rested his back against them. "When I was a little boy, about twelve years old or so, I had a pet bluebird I named Heaven. He used to live outside my window in an old Cypress tree. Every morning he'd make his way over to my windowsill and start talking to me. At first it drove me crazy because he'd wake me up when I wanted to sleep. But eventually he won me over and most of the time I was waiting for him by the window before he arrived."

"We'd sit and talk for a long time each morning. He'd tell me his troubles and I'd tell him mine. If I interrupted him while he was talking he'd just get louder until I stopped. Interruptions for him were a lack of respect and he wouldn't stand for it, friend or no friend. The one time I wouldn't stop interrupting him he just fly back to his nest like I was never there in the first place. I learned respect for others from a bluebird."

"Anyway, one day Heaven stopped showing up. I didn't know just what to think, so I went over to his house to see if anything was the matter. As I was approaching the cypress tree I saw a real small bird on the ground by its trunk. It was too small to be Heaven, but yet it looked just like him. The little bird wasn't moving, but I could see his chest heaving every now and then, so I knew he was alive. Well, I bent down and picked him up. Within seconds I heard Heaven yelling at me, louder than I had ever heard him. I looked up and offered the small bird to him, thinking he just might know what was wrong and be able to help, but he just kept squawking at me. He even landed next to me and almost took a peck at the little guy I had in my hand. That made me mad at him and I covered the little fellow to protect him and took him inside to see if I could help."

July

"I thought I was doing something nice. Over the course of the next several weeks I fed him and gave him water and watched him begin to grow. He became my friend. Each day I waited for Heaven to appear on my windowsill so we could talk about the small bird and each day I was disappointed. He wasn't going to come anywhere near the windowsill. And if I went out to the old cypress he just turned his back on me and wouldn't say a word. I just couldn't understand what was going on."

"In time the little bird was well enough to be returned to the outside. By this time I had figured out that this was Heaven's son. I took him out to the cypress tree he had fallen out of and placed him on a branch and began to walk away, thinking I had helped him to live, given him a second chance of sorts. Within seconds he did what was instinctive for him to do. He leaped from the branch and tried to fly. Problem was, he couldn't. As instinctive as flying should have been to him, more than instinct was needed. He had needed Heaven's guidance on things inherited. He fell to the ground again, this time breaking his wing and his leg. I took him inside again but within a day he died. What I didn't know at that time was that Heaven was there, sitting up in the tree, watching the two of us. All

Jeff Gutterman

that time we had had our little talks on the windowsill he had been trying to tell me how he was going to help his son by allowing him a little instruction and a lot of encouragement and then leaving him alone to learn it on his own. He had been trying to tell me in his way not to interfere in the process, that everything would be okay on its own."

"I thought I was helping. But I hadn't asked permission to do so and help was never asked of me. I just charged right in there thinking I knew what was best, that I could fix everything, rather than leaving him alone to work out his initial challenge with Heaven. It cost my new little friend his life. Once again, a bluebird was my teacher. Allowing people to do for themselves, unless they've specifically asked for my help, has been a lesson I've had to have repeated over and over again before I finally understood it."

"By the time you and I had met, the lesson was so well ingrained in me, that even when I was surrounded with love I refused to act out of fear."

"Fear of rejection and the pain that goes with it is pretty strong, isn't it?"

"It's a pretty silly way to exist."

Chapter Twelve

For three days and three nights the sun and moon had exchanged places in the heavens above. Neither Wheeler nor July had noticed. Their time had been spent inside in a universal black hole. Nothing moved forward, nothing moved backward. Nothing moved at all. They talked and laughed and cried, wandering back through each other's past and the patterns that had made them who they were. Moments turned to centuries had been strung together, end over end as they had embraced and made love a thousand times, each knowing the other's body better than their own. And when the light side of love nudged them, they danced to old tunes they found on the radio.

Both were exhausted, but yet more alive than either could remember. The new awareness of who each actually was had created an energy within them that neither had experienced before. A heightened awareness centered around an inner peace was how July would describe it. The moment was theirs but the hour was drawing near. Outside, for the first time they could remember, came Dakota's howl. Long, startling and formative.

Caught in an unlikely place for a look see, Wheeler shut the shower water off and opened the door. Drenching wet he reached for a couple towels, handing one to July and wrapping the other around himself, and stepped out of the shower.

"Wheeler, wait!"

He turned, glanced and smiled. "Just going to take a look. Sounds like something's up. I've never heard Dakota sound like that before."

"Can't we go together?"

"Sweetie, I'm only going to take a look. I'll be right back."

"Those are famous words around here. Don't you dare go without me!"

97

Together they moved down the hallway through the small house, back toward the kitchen where it had all started three days ago. It seemed to both that with each step their movement slowed and their thoughts floated, waves of energy moving through their bodies at a greater and greater pace.

"Wheeler, I'm scared. Something's happening. This doesn't have a good feel to it."

"We're together. Just keep holding my hand. We're not going to be separated again."

July hadn't heard a word Wheeler had said. The last sound that she had been receptive to was that of Dakota. She had in fact fainted dead away, falling to the floor below. Wheeler's large hand was still holding hers as she hit its wooden surface and thankfully had stilled the fall. He bent to her immediately.

"July! July, wake up sweetie!" He raced to the sink and filled the first thing he found with tap water. Returning to her he started to lower it to her lips, had a second thought and poured it over her face.

Her coughing was quite real. "Wheeler, you're trying to kill me."

He laughed. She laughed. And then the moment before she fainted returned to both of them. They could still hear Dakota. With a glance toward her that everything was going to be okay, Wheeler released his hand behind July's head and moved toward the door.

"I've never fainted before. What's going on? Sam Wheeler, where are you going!"

"We're not going to live in fear."

As he opened the door and stepped through it out of sight, July rose to a sitting position. Her mind was a blank. Thoughts had no entry to her for the moment. She just stared toward the ceiling, closed her eyes and glided over empty space. Time passed for the first time for her since they had found each other again. And slowly a tear left the corner of her eye and made its way across her face.

Forever had passed. She had come out of the black hole. How and why she didn't know. She just knew she had. As she began to stand she had to steady herself by leaning on the kitchen sink. Her knees felt like rubber, her legs trying their best to hold the weight of her body without giving way. Mental cement had been placed on her shoulders pushing her back toward the floor. She didn't want to give in, but the weight was becoming unbearable. She fought to maintain. She won. A moment passed, then another.

When she felt strong enough she made her way to the sink and splashed some water over her face. There was a momentary feeling of freedom as she realized she was standing in the kitchen, her lower body the only part of her wrapped in the towel. Her thoughts flashed back on Wheeler and his expression when he realized that that was all she was going to cover as she stepped from the shower. In her mind's eye she saw his warm, energetic expression as he had looked at her. And it made her laugh and forge others, wondering where all the energy from the two of them kept coming from. And then she snapped back to the present, focused a moment, and realized the contradictions that were now happening. She couldn't hear Dakota anymore but yet Wheeler hadn't returned either. The house was still there, she was still inside it and the lightheadedness had disappeared. If they were separating again, truly separating, then it would make sense that they would both leave the area they had come together in. But that hadn't happened. Alone maybe, but she was still within their kingdom.

Her breathing was becoming regular again. Her intellect had persisted until she had moved beyond her fear. Now she needed to take action. July headed toward the door that Wheeler had moved through a lifetime ago. Stepping just out-side the elements of warm and comfortable, her eyes moved over the landscape of the farm like those of an artist. Each rock or piece of cedar that had been sprinkled around the grounds was taken in. Shrubs and herbs of all kinds moved at the same speed through her vision. The tool shed and greenhouse were scanned with microscopic precision. Wheeler wasn't in sight.

"God Wheeler, where are you? You can't have gone without me. It doesn't work that way and that wasn't part of the deal." Two or three times she shouted his name. All that returned was the sound of the empty wind.

The feeling of defeat was beginning to take hold again. July stepped from the house onto the scattered cedared ground and began to walk. Her eyes didn't leave the surrounding landscape. She could see him everywhere but yet he was nowhere in sight. Once or twice the wind kicked up and she would stop moving, allowing a warm breeze to wind its way around her, causing her eyes to close, her head to tilt toward the sky, and the exhaling of a heavy sigh.

She shuddered in anger at her loss of control, and began clenching and unclenching her fists. And then, as though afraid that the mighty wizard in the sky might be listening and she'd destroy any chance of getting Wheeler back, she ever so softly whispered her mental plea to the wind spirit. "You create magic, I know it. You created it for me, for me, for us. I don't know how we've offended you, but with all my being I'm sorry. Please, please, bring him back."

She listened first and then painstakingly began to open her eyes. "Oh Wheeler. All I can think about is how you've left me again."

"I didn't leave you, you left me, remember?"

July turned around so fast she almost tripped over her own feet.

Coming toward her, Dakota in his arms, was Wheeler. An interesting pair indeed she thought, Wheeler carrying a dog much too big for him, too big for anybody really, and Dakota holding his paws over his nose. She automatically began grinning from ear to ear. But the grin didn't last. At first she began to shake and then completely lost it, broke down and started crying.

Chapter Thirteen

"Sweetie, what in the world's wrong? Are you okay?"

July responded by throwing herself at him, her arms finding their mark around his neck, burying and squishing Dakota between them. The sudden move startled Wheeler who attempted to lower Dakota to the ground. With great effort he deposited their friend between them, stepped over him and returned July's gentle stranglehold.

"Okay, I'm right here. What happened to cause this?"

"You've been gone so long I thought you'd disappeared again. You scared me half to death. I guess I'm just so happy you're still here. I'm sorry."

"Nothing to be sorry about. But you have managed to confuse me."

"What'd you mean?"

"You said that I've been gone a long time."

"You sure were. Don't you think twenty minutes is a long time just to check out a sound?"

"Twenty minutes? Sweetie, I've only been gone about three minutes. What's been going on with you that caused you to think twenty minutes had passed?"

"Three minutes, really? Oh Wheeler, can we sit down please."

With July holding her own head and looking somewhat decomposed, they moved slowly and gently toward the ground, lowering themselves to a space within arms reach of Dakota. Without removing his touch from July, Wheeler reached over and lightly stroked the golden retriever's head.

"I'm sorry. I got so wrapped up in thinking I was losing you again, losing us again, that I had stopped thinking about Dakota's howling. What happened? Why is he covering his nose and what is that awful smell?"

Wheeler took a moment and looked at July, looking so innocent and only part of her wrapped in a towel. He laughed, took her in his arms, and kissed her all over for a very long time. When he pulled back he offered the brightest smile she had seen in awhile.

"He chased something he shouldn't have. It stopped to defend itself by lifting its tail and sending a blaze of uncomfortable deodorant in Dakota's direction. He can't get the smell out of his nostrils."

They both howled until they were no longer sitting on the ground but laying on it. Every now and then they'd glance toward their friend and watch as he tried to rub the invisible intruder out of his nose. That just caused them to laugh harder and louder, both eventually holding their mid sections to keep from hurting anymore then necessary.

"We'd better give him a bath or we're going to be living with that odor for awhile."

"Will soap work?"

"No. But I think I saw some milk in the refrigerator."

"A milk bath? He's not going to like that very much."

"I think you're right. But that's not going to be our main problem. Getting him to forget himself for a minute and follow us into the kitchen is."

They helped each other to their feet and tried unsuccessfully to coax Dakota to move with them. The only acknowledgment he gave them was a quick helpless glance in their direction. When they realized he wasn't going to pay them much attention for the moment they headed in the direction of the kitchen, hoping when he realized that he couldn't help himself he might change his mind and choose to follow. But before they moved ten feet Wheeler came to an abrupt stop, an old wizardly look coming into his eyes.

"It's starting to come together July. I can feel it. It's moving inside me. My whole body's tingling."

"What are you talking about? Did you inherit a few of Dakota's fleas?"

"No, no. You and me. The disappearing and reappearing. Going back and forth through time as though it doesn't exist. The feeling of time standing still. The feeling you had that it was passing very quickly a moment ago. I think I've got some answers. I don't know just how I know all this but it seems right."

Standing now about fifty feet from the side door to the kitchen, Wheeler's thoughts gave way to the light haze of purple sky that was beginning to form before them. Laced with odd shaped white streaks of varying sizes, some seemed to touch the ground only feet from where they stood. It was a sight to behold. July followed Wheeler's glance, her eyes moving as his had, taking in the different colored hues of purple. Dakota, who had been immersed in his own problems and initially refused to budge, had now also glanced toward the sky and immediately rearranged his priorities, quickly picking himself up and moving alongside his friends.

Then, seemingly out of nowhere, a huge hole in the Northern heavens began to open. Small at first and then growing in size, it moved toward them at a snail's pace, yet from where it came they both knew instinctively that its progress toward them was at an incredible speed. Within the hole were the marble-like white streaks that now covered the outer sky. As the hole approached, the two of them could make out what could only be referred to as inner space. The white streaks inside the hole were translucent, invisible eyes with a focused gaze of unfocused or vaporous unsecured shapes, most resembling what could only be described as life-forming molecules.

They held tight to each other, Dakota trying to snuggle between their legs. Wheeler glanced downward at the movement below him, but it was only momentary, returning his view quickly to observe the hole. At first they heard no sound but the closer it came the more the whine of its interior became noticeable. Much like the whirlwind of a hurricane, the sound soon became all encompassing, moving the layers of vacuumed space between them until suction began pulling all of the oxygen around them into its unknown mist. Once again Wheeler quickly glanced down toward Dakota who by now had turned into a throw rug, all four paws stretched to the far reaches of the earth. He needn't of worried about Dakota. As the oxygen began to disappear they both began their own descent to the ground, two dead weights hitting a solid surface knocked out cold.

There was one sound just before they passed out and hit the ground. It was July's weak voice crying out to the spirits in the sky, shouting her disapproval of what was happening. "Nooooooo!!!"

Chapter Fourteen

Her movement startled him as she jerked violently, throwing her head back into the rear of the sofa. Thankfully, the padded cushion acted as a catcher's mitt, softening her backward thrusts at the same time its surface startled her into listlessness. Simple Joe moved the contents of the wooden spoon that he had placed under her nose to awaken her, back to the small bowl next to him. Scratching his head, he couldn't understand how its contents had failed to arouse her from her restless exploration. Within its cradle floated a small sampling of his culinary delights, wisps of aromatic flavorings containing sauces and seasonings of all kinds, including remnants of his undisclosed bluish herb. Finally, he gave in and just gazed down at her, wondering just what kind of torture she was choosing to put herself through. Stretched out on the sofa, her eyes remained closed, staring back at his, as if to suggest the question was rhetorical. He couldn't tell if she was there or not. He just couldn't tell.

Reaching down he put his palm on her forehead and gently stroked, trying to understand what devils were moving within her at the moment. With another violent jerk she began to kick, as though falling from some incredible height, and then in the same sharp movement, stretched her arms gracefully through the depths of space in front of her, as though painting a landscape. Simple Joe looked worried.

"July. July honey. Can you hear me? It's me, your friend, Simple Joe. I don't know where you are, but you're frightening me. Please come back, okay? July."

Nothing. No acknowledgment of any kind. More kicking and additional movements of flailing supple arms. That was it. And then just as suddenly as they had begun, they stopped, a smile spreading quietly across her face. July looked as peaceful as anyone could be. Simple Joe just continued to stare. He was out of his depth and he knew it. This wasn't just the reaction to some simple dream she was having, but something more. Much more. Real or imagined, he knew Wheeler was involved at some level.

The sound of a steam whistle interrupted Simple Joe's thoughts. He looked toward the kitchen and back again at July. She was restful now. She'd be okay for a few more minutes. He picked himself up and headed toward the sound on the stove.

She was floating in an empty sky. At first it had frightened her to death. She had tried screaming but nothing was working. Her voice had taken leave of her body. Kicking was next, but it didn't help either. Not one bit. So she gave in to the uncontrollable and just allowed what was occurring to occur. And after awhile it was okay. So much so in fact that she started to feel that she could touch the air around her. Moving her arms from side to side she noticed that she could indeed affect the streams of circulating air. With each movement of her limbs the air currents around her displaced their holdings with little puffs of invisible gases. She could affect what was happening in some way after all. There was an element of control here. Even if it was only in a very small way. And that made her smile and relax.

The clouds were in front of her one moment and beyond her the next. Movement faster than a thought. She didn't understand it but it was comfortable and in some way soothing. It was as though she was being renewed. And she thought "It's about time." And then at that same moment that the thought presented itself, a quiver went through her, a quiver that seemed to talk faster than the speed of light. All at once. Hundreds of words. Not spoken really, just known as an essence.

For a moment she flashed on Wheeler, not in a sad way but to link into an acknowledgment. She remembered his comment about beginning to understand. Something coming all at once to him, a kind of knowing. Now, she was beginning to understand what he meant. But her knowing was hazy, not really defined like she was used to, after she'd had a chance to kick the words and their meaning around a bit. And then Wheeler began to fade, too quickly leaving her mind as she began falling and kicking again, trying to regain control of her thoughts.

She felt frustrated and baffled. Her ego flashed unseen before her, telling her to gain control and everything would be okay. It wasn't a great feeling and intuitively she knew it wasn't right. Not being able to remember, while at the same time still understanding that a moment ago she had, and that it was real and emotionally charged. So she lashed out. This time though the kicks were stronger. So much so that she jerked her body beyond the range of her earlier flight, such a powerful force within her. Finally, with nothing but sheer determination and force, she opened her eyes and began to reorient to physical reality. The first focused visual was Simple Joe's grinning face. The two of them just stared at each other for a long moment, neither attempting beyond their silence to communicate.

Wheeler thought he was in a dream, not a vortex. He was awake but yet everything appeared so ethereal. His memory was sharp, refusing to lose focus of July or Dakota. His mind floated between them at lightning speed. He thought he could almost hear July shouting that she understood. And yet there was another voice in the background. Someone else was calling out to her. There was no threat here and he knew she was okay, but the voice. He'd heard the voice before. Somewhere before. The more he tried to remember, the more frustrated he became. There was something about it. Familiarity, good, bad, something.

He began to relax, giving in. Knowing full well that fighting to understand wasn't going to work. Primal motion forged in any direction was only going to frustrate him further.

He tried desperately to remember the pattern. They were alone. They were together. They came apart. And then found each other again. And once more the wheel moved, the circle opened, the circle closed. Apart. Together. Now apart again. The gods of memory forcing each of them into renewal, over and over again. Wheeler thought he understood. And then he didn't. But he could feel it there all the time. The knowing. That tender, elusive constant. "Face it Wheeler," he kept telling himself. "It's only me reminding me," he shouted to anyone who would listen. "There's no fear here. There's no reason for it." *Move with it Wheeler,* he thought. *Understand it. Make it work for you. Make it work for you and July.*

The voice again. He was hearing the voice in the background again. Soft, barely audible. He listened carefully. "July. July honey. Can you hear me? It's me, your friend, Simple . . ." The voice trailed off, not completing its signature, fading in and out, allowing him to hear bits and pieces of what was being said.

"You're frightening me. Please come back, okay? July."

He listened and then listened again, the same verbal vibration kept repeating itself, over and over again. With each repetition he tensed more. He knew the voice and the energy attached to it. He simply couldn't trace the electrical patterns in his mind for identification. He forced every psychic muscle in his being to reach out to test the ether. Where was the sound coming from? Who was attached to it? What was the relationship with July?

He noticed for the first time that he was moving. Physically paralyzed, he was moving. His being was floating down a long corridor of lights. No walls. No encasements of any kind, yet he knew it to be a passageway. Movement through a never-ending stream of incredible golden white pulsating lights. His thoughts returned. "Was he dead? Is this what everyone had talked about happening when they passed over? The tunnel. The lights."

The voice was gone. The lights were dimming. He had landed. He struggled to expand in every way he could. On his back, flat on the

ground, he opened his mouth and yawned. Next
he stretched. Limbs reaching out in all directions
for an invisible surge of energy to reignite the
body Wheeler. He yawned again and found that
his eyes were watering. He felt he'd fallen into a
deep sleep, the recipient of a thousand dreams
scattering in all directions upon his awakening.

Wheeler sat up and looked around.
Familiarity fought for control over his awakening
confusion and disorientation. He was in a
meadow enveloped on each side by the gentle
slope of wavering grassy hills. The blades were a
light green and contrasted nicely as they curved
up at the highest point of the hills to touch the
crystal blue of the daytime sky. A smile spread
across Wheeler's face as he took in the openness
around him. He exhaled and then took in a deep
breath to sharpen his senses. Closing his eyes he
remained a statue for minutes, the smile never
leaving his lips.

He felt clear. Clearer than he had in years.
There was no past, no present, no future. No
cobwebs, no old noise. No new thoughts, no
projections. Just a state of being and he was
enjoying it. Open for the first time to the music of
the spheres. It was magical and his being was
anointed and pulled in. With each lyrical note
Wheeler began to sway, taking in the melody of

perfect vibratory resonance. When he opened his eyes he could still hear it. Softly it moved on the wings of the wind, continuing to offer him the opportunity to disengage further. But he couldn't. He was starting to remember. And the more she came into view the more he began to feel a surge beneath him.

The land he sat on, as though picking up the harmony of the musical measure around him, began to move. Silently at first, as though searching for just the right entrance and then beginning a rolling cadence from his point of connection, rippling outward from him as though a pebble had been thrown into a quiet pool of water. It seemed the more intense his focus on July, the more excited and severe the ground around him became. He couldn't control it. It seemed that all of his thoughts had completely converged on her and the events that had just recently taken place. But the thrusts of nature had their way, causing Wheeler's heart to beat beyond its capacity for July, moving him into the depths of an escalating fear.

Chapter Fifteen

Five months had passed. Neither Wheeler nor July heard from the other. Empty space and quiet time. Memories remained strong, thoughts of each other touching their individual worlds from moment to moment. But time moved at its own pace, apparently against them, and their belief in finding one other again began to fade. Coming together once in a lifetime was incredible. Twice, maybe with a lot of luck. A third time, seemingly impossible. A fourth, fantasy.

Wheeler finally made it to the Montana range and the wild horses. Along with Dakota they had set up camp at the base of the smallest mountain surrounding the range. For as far as the eye could see, the Valley of the Horses was before them. Split almost down the center by a less than formidable stream, it stilled the wildest heart. The terrain was as smooth as silk, the grass tall, tinged by the sun and made golden brown. With just the right amount of knolls and ground recession, the meadow projected a passive whitecap effect. And on the flatlands between them, old oaks and gentle pines grew spotted and silent as they graced the remaining landscape.

Wheeler had been right. The nights had proven cold and at times angry. But the endurance was worth every chill that made its way through his body. For the first week neither of them saw the horses and close to the end of that time he had almost called it quits. But then they came. Hundreds of them. All shapes, all sizes, all colors. Their thunder moved the mountains and changed the course of the less than formidable stream. Ground hogs dived for the safety of their homes or those of a neighbor, hopefully friendly, as the ground beneath them rippled with its explosion. A pair of bobcats in the area raced to the outer fringes of the range, as they felt the force of an army bearing down on them. And eagles and old hawks perched on the branches of the surrounding trees, quietly took to the sky, smartly avoiding a wall of dust heading toward them.

Their leader was a great stallion, his mane long, lifted by the wind as he ran. Muscular and powerful he wound his way between and betwixt the knolls of the range, toward an apparent pre-determined destination. As fast as he moved, at times separating himself from those that followed, it was easy to see that the majority of his cast was pure white. But there was a minor exception that made him stand out from the brigade he led. Reaching from the farthest point at each ankle, extending upward for the shortest distance, were ribbons of golden wheat, blending perfectly with the landscape he moved through. With white above and below the strands, anyone watching him move would swear that he never touched the ground, his shadow trying to keep up, moving over the land as though floating above it. He was Wheeler's favorite. He had named him Fortune.

Each day for those next several weeks the horses would move through the range at day-break, pausing occasionally to drink from the less than formidable stream. And each day they came closer and closer to the pair of campers but always stopped short of them. The only communication was Dakota's bark as they passed by.

Wheeler tried approaching Fortune at the beginning of the third week only to be disappointed. And that puzzled him, for it was Fortune that had made the initial gesture toward Wheeler. But frustration be damned, Wheeler stayed the course.

For the next month as everyone's trust grew and he was allowed closer, Wheeler took hundreds of photographs of the animals. Especially Fortune. And by the end of the second month he was painting from both the photographs he had developed and what lay before him. He'd never been so focused before. Nothing disturbed his thoughts. Fortune, the other horses, the range, his painting, and the clear air he took in with each breath, wouldn't release him, even to July. And it was another several months before he realized it.

After five months he had become so obsessed with the freedom he saw before him, he failed to notice a man on horseback approaching from the far side of the range. When he finally noticed the advance it wasn't the rider who caught his eye but rather the horse. Not a large horse but then not very small either. Brown. Solid brown. A smaller version of Wildfire. His gait was steady and slow, that of a show horse bred for the range. Gentle, but full of fire, always in command. He seemed familiar, but Wheeler couldn't make the match.

Tall and lean like Wheeler, the man rode as though he were part of the horse. The horse's gait moved him up and down but the gazing eye couldn't catch it. Floating or gliding as they moved forward over the range, the separation of man and beast was impossible to spot. Still a distance from Wheeler's camp, they stopped at the less than formidable stream. As he relaxed the reins and dismounted, he allowed his friend to drink his fill. Pulling a handkerchief from his back pocket he bent to the water and swiped it several times through its clearness. He then dislodged the hat that had shaded his face by the purposeful movement of bowing his head forward into his waiting hand. As he straightened back up he wiped his brow first with his handkerchief and then followed the movement with his sleeve. Then he squinted into the distant sun, blinked once or twice and then lowered his head and stared straight at Wheeler.

Much too far to see each other clearly they stared at the other's image through distant space. The light hair on the back of Wheeler's neck stood erect. Chills raced through his body. He floated as a wave of energy moved within the hollow of his inner mind, causing him to physically back up as though an invisible plate of glass was heading straight toward him. But then he found his center, steadied himself and refocused on the man and the horse. He knew them both, but they were too far in the distance to make out.

"Dakota, come look at this. We've got friends approaching . . . I just hope they're good friends."

Time ran its normal course, the sun moving off its center at the high point in the sky. Wheeler continued to paint, constantly aware of the rider approaching. Years seemed to pass before the brown horse found its way into Wheeler's encampment. With a final brush stroke to the canvas, Wheeler looked up to match the gaze of the man on horseback. Without a sound of introduction they both reviewed the other. Neither spoke.

Wheeler was the first to release his eyes from the stranger. Falling just a few feet and then readjusting for a wider view, they took in the horse. Smaller than the distance had allowed his initial judgment, he felt both surprise and comfort. He had been wrong. His silent new friend wasn't mounted on a stallion but rather a mare. And every inch of her was radiant.

"Her name's Darby. A real beauty isn't she?"

Wheeler returned his gaze to the stranger once again. The voice, he knew the voice. For a second time today he found himself involuntarily backing up to avoid a collision with the advancing invisible glass shield. With his back against the air, he squinted as though hit by a blinding streak of sunlight, trying hard to focus more clearly on the man's words. Darby was the horse's name. Darby! The name raced through Wheeler's mind touching every corner of his soul, pushing Fortune, the herd and his painting into another dimension. Beads of sweat began forming on Wheeler's forehead, the moisture seemingly torn from the sudden dryness in his mouth.

"And yours?"

The stranger was carefully appraising him and he knew it. He was older than Wheeler by a good twenty-five years, his face cut with lines of age that only a human displays. He took him in, all of him. And then he smiled and straightened up.

"You're Wheeler?"

"Yes."

The stranger slowly dismounted, lowered his head to remove his hat, and then held out a hand in front of him. "Name's Simple Joe and I've come a long way to meet you."

Chapter Sixteen

In the soft hours of the morning the air is crisp and clean, the sky, clear and easy on the eyes, tints of light blue meshed with white soft puffs blending into its expansiveness. From above this magnificent global speck, if we moved back in time to the beginning, we could follow the birth of rivers, streams and mighty oceans, and over an extended period, the shifting and settling of mountains and valleys. Some maintained life, some refused it. But all shared the beauty of instant evolutionized creation over time.

The canyon ran deep. Over a mile in length and half a football field wide, with a depth easily over twice its width. The indentation in the earth gave the impression of that of a huge mother ship, having tilted on its side and slid halfway into the earth's crust. As though having been shaved with a fine razor, the walls of the canyon were as smooth as silk. No protrusions, no jagged edges, no holes. There were peaks and hollows but they resembled the higher and lower portions a piece of cloth blowing in the wind might make. The abyss had been around for thousands of years. July had discovered it for the first time several months after having moved to the area.

At a shepherd's pace she walked its floor. Unlike its walls, the path beneath her resembled a rough, uncut diamond with only spotted clarity. Stones of varying sizes, some whole, most only a portion of who they used to be, these split into dissimilar shapes. It was these fragments that held and focused a portion of July's attention. The water that seemed to wrap itself around the stones as it moved, accounted for the remainder. From out of nowhere it flowed effortlessly, winding and weaving its way from an unknown source, over the canyon floor to some mystical destination.

In shorts and tennis shoes, July moved cautiously through unfamiliar territory. She had only traveled this way once before and that now seemed a lifetime ago. Slowly and casually she'd skate the floor of the canyon with simple uncertain steps, moving forward a little only to stop and glance around her, unsure of herself in a way she couldn't remember. The setting was light, the brilliant rays of sunshine at high noon covering every spindle of sand from one end of the canyons rainbow to the other. But her thoughts were obscure, first unraveling and then coming together, moving in unison with her footsteps. Thinking back over her life, almost to the beginning, always caused an ebb and flow of emotions.

An only child, her family was her entire world her first several years of life. Farm people. Close to the earth. They touched each other's hearts often, each to the other, their extended family and their friends. But growing up happened all too soon. When she was five she was playing with imaginary dolls and at six an evolved adult with the loss of her father. At fourteen she discovered the opposite sex. She couldn't remember his name and could now just barely see the outlines of his face, but she caught the momentary feeling of emotions that infatuation had allowed. At twenty-two it was a bittersweet year. Her first love, warm and tender, tempered in a moments time by the loss of her mother and what remaining family she had left. The thought cast a magical spell over her, holding her in the past, refusing her mind the ability to move forward. A tear then a sigh, followed by a mellow smile.

When the moment lifted she glanced down, caught herself almost ankle deep in the stream, searched her inner mind for something silly and then just laughed. Throwing her head back, involving her entire being in her now jovial self, she noticed above her a family of free floating parrots that seemed to ride the air currents the mild canyon winds provided.

"Hey guys. You're beautiful! Where'd you come from?"

An attempt at communication as one of them glanced down at her words and rode the sun's streams of light in front of her, coming close enough to exaggerate her smile even further. She now moved and twisted her body in whatever direction necessary to follow the flight of her new companion. And as she desired it he sensed her thought and once again moved on the invisible path before her, circled her completely and then held himself still and silent in the air, slowly coming to rest on her waiting shoulder.

"No fear, huh?"

At the same time she had located a large boulder to sit on, her hand had moved to coax him onto it. With the tilt of his head and a gaze through the physical and into her soul, he followed her lead. In the blink of an eye they were old friends.

"I don't know what your name is, but I think I'll call you Darian. I don't know why, it just sounds right. You've got faith. You're open and trusting and I like that. Maybe you can teach me."

As she talked with Darian her eyes fell on every part of him. Beautiful yet strange markings for a parrot. A tinge of yellow there, a spot of pale white over here, both laid over him onto a background of light green, while sky blue lightning rod like streaks made their way in very thin engravings toward his tails end. Noticing nature's writing, July moved her head even closer to the hand Darian sat on, eyes locked on his tail.

"My God."

The thin, sky blue colored lines she noticed were initials. Although somewhat ragged they definitely formed the letters S. W., an engraving that brought immediate recognition. Was she seeing things, letting her imagination run away with her thoughts. Sam Wheeler. She hadn't thought of contact with Wheeler again until just now. She had accepted what she had considered to be her fate. Now she wasn't so sure.

"Darian, where did you and your friends come from? And don't just tilt your handsome head and look at me with those mystical eyes.

What other markings do your friends have on them?"

July lifted her head to locate Darian's friends but the movement was in vain. Darian was alone. Now her heart raced.

"Darian, talk to me."

He did. He responded by bobbing his head in an up and down fashion in much the same way Wheeler would have answered in the affirmative. And then, Darian's movement ceased. He looked straight into July's eyes, holding her vision with an unseen mental process. At first he just squinted and fluttered his paper thin eyelids at her. Then he closed his eyes to encompass her in his warmth, granting her a Merlin-like view of life. Magically and unceremoniously he locked onto the mirror beyond her beautiful green eyes, tilted his head and wouldn't let go. July floated, her eyes moving her mind into another time, her mind's memory aroused once again, surging back through non-dimensional space to her past. Wheeler was momentarily lost, left in a holding pattern, not yet fully allowed to inhabit her mind. She instinctively knew that her longing for answers lay within.

Her mind moved well beyond its capable speed. She was thirty and beautiful, her physical outline graced by the hands of an artist. She remembered being open, trusting, wild and spontaneous with life, following her heart in all that she did. The energy she put out was the energy she attracted. People. Situations. Opportunities. Growth. Instinctively she could sense it. Emotionally she could feel it. It was a great time of life. A year shy of meeting Wheeler for the first time.

Friends seemed to come and go, nothing was permanent. Maybe that was it. Maybe people were supposed to just come and go, keeping their before-life agreements to touch at some point in space and time for awhile before moving on. When we need someone they're there. When we've grown beyond our creation they go. Or we do. Permanency enhances comfort and effortlessness and both have a way with most of inhibiting the spontaneous, the free-flow of creation, the heartfelt trust and inner knowing. Constant change within self motivated parameters is the only way of constant growth, of moving along the back roads of the process itself, the reason for being. It was coming to her that her need for Wheeler had provided a lack of trust in herself, an indigence of faith. It wasn't Wheeler's lack of telling her he loved her that had made her go, it was a lack in herself. A deficit in the thought process a long time ago.

There was an inner feeling of darkness, clouds and rain. And then the trance lifted and she saw the sunlight smiling and anxious. With a mighty breath she shouted to the Wind God, "Yes!" July threw Darian up into the sky and began dancing. "Wheeler, we are going to meet again! And it couldn't have happened until now. It was my lack of understanding that kept pulling us back and forth in every direction. I needed to understand, to have the knowing you said you thought you were getting. I've got it and it's powerful! Now Wheeler, now. Come for me now!"

From below the earth's crust a response was sent toward her. Originating always from its center to the upper portion of its outer rim, the energy circulated a thousand times through sand, rocks and immovable strata before reaching its target. The gods were happy and they were sending their thoughts to her to let her know. The floor of the canyon began to shift. Two dusty horizontal escalators moving in opposite directions, stopping and starting over and over, dancing the dance of a new beginning.

July was thrown off balance, slipped and fell trying to regain her footing, hitting her head on the soft mushy wall of the canyon. As she was falling she tried to scream but time wouldn't allow it. Even with its pulpy softness the impact was forceful enough to knock her to the ground unconscious. At first there was nothing, but then the darkness began to color the page in her mind.

She was dreaming. His raincoat was dark blue, made of a cloth-like material. Each pellet of water that touched its surface rolled into a ball and fell to the ground. Hers was a light ivory color, shorter in length than his, lighter in weight. When the wind off the Sound touched its thread, it moved through it to the lining below, chilling her body to the bone. They stood quietly on the deck of the ferry, neither wanting to speak first, each feeling the warm glow of passion building within them. But touching was impossible, even in a light downpour. They were being watched and they knew it.

For four days and four nights they had tried to avoid them, moving through a sequence of unseen corridors, opening and closing the doors that moved them from one place to the other. Nothing had worked. They were to be denied the passion they felt for each other. If they were to live, it would have to remain unexpressed. That was the agreement. Simple but painful. On one level they had merely forgotten they had made it.

Behind them on an upper deck of the ferry he watched and they knew it. He had been with them since the beginning. No peace, no privacy.

Only talking. That was all that was allowed. Their punishment had been brutal, but so had their crime. Three other times in lives gone by they had known each other. Three other times they had fallen in love but had been afraid to take the chance. To express themselves. Fully and completely. Each life time they had been pulled together at some point in time with regard to some circumstance that had been set for them. They had talked and made love, exposing the other in every way possible. They had held hands at sunset and been entwined in the morning light. Everything and anything. Over and over again. But in the end they hadn't committed to each other. Fear over love. A bad choice. There wouldn't be a fourth time. This time the attraction would be there but beyond the visual and emotional, any consummation wouldn't be allowed. They may forge forward to understand it but understanding wouldn't ease the pain. Beyond that the memories would return, full force, much like a raging river, flooding their essence with their past fears and failures.

She awoke with a shiver, a parrot on her breast staring down at her. "Darian, my God what a dream. If that's what it was?"

Chapter Seventeen

In a field on the other side of forever, an open range at the base of a small mountain, sat two men. Off to one side raged a small circular fire, occasionally fanned by the gentle wind of the surrounding area. Every so often, when the flames became submissive, one of the men could be persuaded to reach out beyond their immediate environment and locate some additional brush and prickled cacti to continue its magic. About two feet across, its warmth of yellowish-orange colors stretched just far enough beyond its borders to supply both the men with some relief from the cool nighttime air.

They had been talking for hours, each fascinated by the other, it seemed old friends from an age forgotten, meeting for the first time. Earlier, as Simple Joe had dismounted and held his hand to Wheeler, Wheeler's response had been automatic, silently offering his in return, the back of his mind pushing forward to completely capture the name Simple Joe. Somewhere, in the deepest wells of his being it held meaning, but identification eluded him. As they clasped hands the review of each other was more panoramic, each going the distance, searching deeply into the others soul. What passed between the two men is written on the wind, but it's fair to say that there was a mutual knowing of the other. Then Wheeler glanced beyond Simple Joe's image to that of Darby's.

"If you'll get the harness I'll remove the saddle and we can let her run." And so it was. Wheeler reaching up to remove the harness, Simple Joe unfastening the saddle.

"She's beautiful. The name, Darby. I know the name."

Simple Joe once again took in the measure of the man before him before he spoke. "She's one of a kind. The minds memory creates wonderful pictures, doesn't it?"

A silent movement in the wind, nothing more than a breeze, and there stood a large white stallion with ribbons of golden wheat shooting through his ankles. Darby turned and locked onto Fortune. Nudging her at first with his head she responded, and within a moments time both raced out into the night and onto the open range, moving toward the untamed stable of companions that awaited them.

"She'll return for you?"

"Maybe, maybe not. Darby's always been free. The lady who owns her believes in invisible fences. She's always been free to come and go.

"The lady that owns her?"

Simple Joe just smiled. He knew. A few seconds, a few minutes. Wheeler would tune in if he hadn't already. And he was right.

At first his brow wrinkled and then he smiled. The smile was country size and genuine. "In the back of my mind I knew someone would come. Didn't know who or why, but for months now just had a feeling about it."

"And in some way I knew I was expected."

"How is she?"

"When I left she was a little confused. Was choosing to spend more and more time by herself."

Wheeler bowed his head and for a moment silently told her he loved her and that somehow and someway they'd be together again soon. "I've heard a lot about you. You've been a good friend to her. Thank you."

"It's me that should thank you. You give us a lot to talk about."

They both laughed, any distance remaining between them now closed. At first they talked of worldly things, both taking their time before entering the depth of emotional realties that they had really come together for. Wheeler not sure he had complete answers, Simple Joe unsure of what he could provide. Simple Joe's hat was a topic, a Stetson with a small bullet hole in its rear, patched with a piece of plaid patterned cotton. Wheeler's boots came up once, a discussion around the two puncture marks on the stem of one of them and what occurred to the snake that made them. Then of painting, photography, and ranching in that order. The dinner they ate became a topic of discussion, a combination of praise and gentle moans when something hit the taste buds just right. People they'd known, old friends and acquaintances who somehow had left their mark, either in a passing moment or over the long span of years that time had stretched for them. There was a knowing between the two men that the lives they'd lived had overlapped, a comfortable yet unsettled familiarity with the spirit of each other.

As the meal was settling within them, Simple Joe took a pipe and some tobacco from an inside jacket pocket. Wheeler watched as he pinched just the right amount of tobacco from its pouch, lifted it and then stuffed it into the bowl of the pipe. Reaching for a nearby twig, Wheeler passed it through the fire, the thinnest part of the branch of a tree, strong and passively pulsating with life at one time, now holding a flame on the tip of its limb. The overture was expected as Simple Joe leaned into the plume, sucked comfortably and lit the pipe. No thank you's or you're welcome's, just the look of approval one man to the other, both of them knowing it was time to talk of more important things.

Wheeler was the first to open the sealed jar. "You've come a long way."

"I have a dear friend who claims to have traveled distances far longer than mine."

"Yes, I'd say that's fair. An unmeasured distance is always the farthest."

"So it's true?"

Wheeler looked into the distance before he spoke. "Sand hills."

"Don't understand."

"Mountains can be negotiated. You know they're solid and your footing's secure. But when the reality you're playing in has its foundation made of sand, each time you make a movement you're not sure if one of you will disappear if it shifts. It seemed that every time we thought we were on firm ground, the grains beneath us moved and swallowed us up, forcing us in different directions."

Simple Joe's head was bowed, nodding in agreement as Wheeler had talked. And then he looked up, matching his eyes and marking his heart and responded, nothing that needed verbalization but there it was, out in the open. "The power of love is pretty strong. She's never left her home yet she's been with you several times now. Desire takes us where we want to be no matter where we are. I'll admit I had my doubts when she first started telling me what was going on. Being here, being there, being back here again. I'd forgotten just how strong we were to be able to create whatever we really want."

"As much as I understand what you're saying, I'll tell you that that's also the part that's confusing to me. If we came together again by both desiring it then why isn't she here right now? Why were we pulled apart again?"

"July feels comfortable with me. Tells me I remind her of her father a little. And, if I was able to admit the truth to myself, she reminds me of the daughter that I lost many years ago. I guess you could say that there's a kind of symbiosis between us. Maybe that's why she shares so freely with me. And that's what it is, it's sharing, not confiding. Wheeler, you and I don't know each other well . . . but then again maybe we do . . . stop me if I'm intruding, but if you'll allow it, a comment from someone who's climbed the mountains and visited the sand traps before, although admittedly, with a very different kind of sand."

"I'm comfortable with you. And I think you've come a long way to help July and in turn that helps both of us. Ask what you feel you need to and say what you will. No intrusion taken. I do have a question though before you begin."

Simple Joe took a long drag on his pipe and slowly blew the smoke into the air over their heads. "No, she's not aware I came looking for you. Although we have no real secrets from each other I simply suggested that I needed to get away for awhile and asked if she minded if I borrowed Darby back. Actually I wasn't sure I could even find you."

Wheeler should have been surprised but he wasn't. The question could have been anticipated. "Borrowed Darby back?"

"Darby was once mine. When I met July I knew she was to be hers. I tried to give her to her but she wouldn't have any of that. So we set a fair price and she purchased her."

"That's an expensive horse!"

"You're right. And she's still paying her off. One home cooked meal monthly and a captive audience for my stories."

They laughed together, the new friendship secure within itself. Their comfort level with each other seemed to grow with each passing wave of the night mist, causing even the brightest star to appear as a rainbow of colored light.

In July's world it was still daylight. She put the book down, rocked a bit in her chair and looked down at her wooden porch. Reaching for a writing tablet she made some notes every once in a while, scanned the sky in an empty unknown search, and spoke to anyone who just might be listening. "I can't help but wonder were he went. It's not like Joe to just take off the way he did.

Especially without sharing where he was going. It's just not like him."

From far off a tumbleweed blew onto the steps of the porch, held its position gathering some ground dust, and then lifted a few feet into the air and flew half a football field away. She picked her book back up, closed her eyes and opened it to an arbitrary page. A smile spread across her face and made her lips tilt in that wonderful way that suggested that there was something significant in what she had just read. She closed her eyes, took a deep breath and refocused on the words: *"In an age when all things are possible, we deceive ourselves by granting emotion to the thoughts of parameters and limitations. We continually short circuit an already overburdened mental switchboard with thoughts of flight from our self-created restrictions. All we have to do to have anything we really want, is to think it into already being and believe it is so. It's really all so simple."*

Delighted, she closed the book and reopened it to another passage. This time she added a nod and some tears to the thought, *"We are all connected, each to the other, equally. However, the stronger the emotion of the relationship, the closer the connection. This is not a contradiction. Lives are shared many times over throughout our various sojourns in the multiplicity of realities. We come together, we move apart, but never the heart. This is the one area that we continue to hold each other's essence—until reunification, which will always happen. And at times, if our energy is confused and stagnant because we make it so, another energy may join with ours to help the flow begin again."*

July stared into the vastness of the unseen stars in the heavens and then silently shouted to herself, "That's it! I know where Simple Joe went!"

It took forever to track down the phone numbers, most of which were in stored boxes that she had up in the attic. Then, with growing anticipation, she made the calls. Old friends, close to both of them at one time, now just familiar voices traveling through an invisible continuum, dancing over copper wires through the distance of geographical boundaries for hundreds and hundreds of miles. Pleasant surprises and answers laced with a great deal of uncertainty was her reward for the first several hours. No one had seen Wheeler in quite awhile. Heartbroken, she was about to call it quits, ready to admit defeat, when something told her to turn around. Glancing in the direction the silent command had come from, she turned and saw two familiar white doves landing on the windowsill.

The motivation was back. She reached into the carton she had brought down from the attic, fumbled through its contents one more time, finally producing a wrinkled piece of paper from its interior. Smiling, she dialed the number written on its surface. The friendly voice at the other end presented her with the gold mine she had been looking for. Through a series of comments and possibilities that the conversation had emitted, she thought she had a pretty good handle on where he was and where Simple Joe had gone. She knew deep in her heart that Simple Joe loved her like a daughter, and would do anything in his power to help her understand what was going on between her and Wheeler. Failing that, lacking the understanding himself, he would have set out to find Wheeler.

She gathered several pairs of jeans, sweaters and jackets, throwing them all into the back of her car, now covered nicely front to back with dust from not having been moved for the last month. Then, she made some sandwiches, bits of this and that, and tossed them into several plastic containers. Along with several bottles of water and a beer or two, everything went into a fairly large cooler that was placed alongside the jeans. This wasn't going to be a three day trip. She would do it in one straight run. Excited, she climbed in, turned the key and got about fifteen feet before realizing that one of the tires wasn't going to accommodate her. It took almost an hour hunting for tools to change the tire with before she realized where she'd put them. Another half an hour and she was on the road.

As she hit the main highway there wasn't another vehicle in sight. The road seemed to belong to her. In a good mood, smiling and visualizing being with Wheeler, she was also wondering if Simple Joe had actually found him and how long they'd been together, what they'd talk about and if they'd like each other. The thought caused her to broaden her smile even more. Of course they'd like each other. A hundred miles out she was lost in her friends, only vaguely aware of her speed before she heard the siren, looked in her rearview mirror and saw the flashing red lights.

Chapter Eighteen

"Well, it's hard to say. I think I've got a handle on it . . . but then again . . . don't really know."

"Wheeler, part of the reason I made this trip is because I've got something to share with you. Needs to be shared with July also but I've held off with her. I know how she likes to ask questions . . . a take it apart, understand why it ticks and then put it back together kind of person. I didn't have the answers for her. I've never been able to gain them for myself. And I thought sharing this with her at this point, with all that's happened to her . . . to you and her . . . wouldn't have been very beneficial without them. At first I thought what I had would be helpful and maybe, just maybe, you and I together could pull the pieces of this thing into some understandable design."

"What's happened to July and me . . . it's happened to you before?"

The sun seemed to circle the earth in the time it took Simple Joe to attempt an answer. Wheeler wasn't the type of man that was surprised or scared easily, but he held Joe's gaze with an anticipation he couldn't remember.

"How about another cup of coffee?"

His spell was broken. ". . . Sure." Wheeler started to pour what was left of the liquid into Joe's thermos cup when the ground beneath them began to shake. Mildly at first, growing in intensity, at last throwing both men to the ground. Between them a crack had appeared. A ragged line drawn in the earth. At first they were pulled toward each other, only inches apart. Then, before either could gain a stance, they were vaulted in opposite directions, Simple Joe flung in the open space behind where he had been sitting a moment before, and Wheeler catapulted a hundred and eighty degrees away from him. The inches between them had quickly turned to feet and the feet to yards, first one, then two, then ten, all with laser like speed. Then, as if the distance between the two men hadn't separated them enough, the earth belched again. The ground Wheeler was on began to rise, slowly at first, then with a thrust upward that caused an almost upright Wheeler to hit the hard earth a second time. Now there was a distance of light years between the two.

While Wheeler's movement was toward the heavens, he was keenly aware that Simple Joe's was into the earth. As the burps continued, drawn it seemed from somewhere deep within the belly of the planet, a somewhat weary yet excited Wheeler attempted to gain what control he could. With desperation in his voice he called out to his new friend. "Joe, can you hear me?" Nothing. What with the roar of the earth's crust moving against itself, the sound of a human voice was not to be heard. "Joe," he shouted in vain. Whether he was still with him and unable to answer or now in another world, Wheeler had no way of knowing.

For a time the sound grew louder before moving into a whisper. Then, as if a magic wand had been waved over the land, this mass of tightly bundled dirt and rocks fell silent. When it finally stopped, Wheeler reached for the jagged dividing line, the rim of the edge of the earth that jutted out into open space. Knowing now that his weight was suspended on only a small portion of dirt, he carefully bent forward, leaned over and looked down. Nothing but the depths of blackness. Simple Joe had completely disap-peared, a quick survey also suggesting the disappearance of his easel, many of his paints, and Stanley. What he was thankfully left with was Dakota, a few cans of food, the empty paint box and the two sleeping bags that had kept them both warm throughout the night.

———————————

July was having her own problems. The tickets were piling up. Not intentionally, but there they were. She would become so focused on Wheeler and Simple Joe that she was oblivious to her immediate surroundings. She was driving on the road okay, could maneuver if called for or necessary, but the speed at which she moved from here to there wasn't part of her mental process. There were times she approached the place on the speedometer where two zeroes ran together without realizing it. Three tickets on the seat beside her, but once again she was focused and flying.

All of a sudden she forced her whole body further into the seat, and within seconds slowed by slamming on the brakes and pulling to the side of the road. "My God!"

July

July had a visual of Wheeler and Simple Joe move before her. She saw the quake just as it happened, the separation in the ground, the widening chasm between the two men, and then Simple Joe's disappearance. From that, her vision went black. Nothing. Absolutely nothing. Her heart beat uncontrollably and for a moment she felt as though it would be ripped from her chest. She'd had somewhat the same feeling in the restaurant with Wheeler. This was worse. She knew she was completely alone. Slowly she removed herself from the car. Fresh air. She needed fresh air.

The light that comes with the rising sun was reaching toward the prone bodies of Wheeler and Dakota. But without the gift of a breeze to carry its warmth, its gentle touch disturbed neither man nor beast. An hour passed, the sun's rays now shooting beams of filtered light through an invisible starry universe. They were beginning to warm the cloud cover, its blanket containing the generated heat from its origin. Slowly, from the depths of another reality, their dream state began to extend beyond their focus and the two of them were pulled back to the physicality around them.

Wheeler's arm stretched to the morning sky. Dakota's hind leg extended behind him. An arm, a leg and then shortly the eyes. Both were once again becoming aware of the other. Another movement of time and they were back in their physical environment. Remembering the earth's movement and all that had occurred a few hours before, Wheeler was somewhat uncomfortable, "Boy have we got a mess on our hands" was Wheeler's verbal good morning to Dakota.

Only a few feet from the crest of the ledge, Wheeler slowly turned over and crawled to its side. Peering over all he could see was emptiness. Allowing his head to actually extend beyond the ledge, he looked down and then behind it, into total blackness under where he was laying. He extended his arm to its farthest reach beneath and under him. When he finally touched the earth he jerked his hand back with startling speed. "Jesus, Mother of God." Quickly Wheeler backed away from where he had been positioned, pushing himself a foot at a time until there was a good ten to fifteen feet between himself and the edge. Dakota, sensing Wheeler knew what he was doing, followed suit.

A subtle fear began to settle over him and sweat trickled down his face. Then, without the ability to control it, a sense of loss rippled through his body, causing him to shake. At first his hands made little back and forth movements. Then the body tremor moved up his arms. His thighs were next, the strongest part of his body bowing to the intensity of his invisible emotions. It wasn't just the quake. It was the loss of a new friend that he now knew he had known for eons. And of course there was July. Beautiful July.

It went on for the better part of a quarter hour, leaving him more drained and exhausted than the previous night's actual events. When all had quieted he drew a huge breath of air, filling his lungs to capacity and released it as though it was his final act on earth. And then the scene repeated itself several more times. When he finally felt settled he sat up and looked around.

With all that had happened, all the movement, all the noise, everything looked the same. Even the range below where the horses ran free remained untouched. Everything was the same except the marked division that had separated Simple Joe and himself.

One more time he lay on his stomach and crawled over to the ledge and looked down. And one more time he backed away. "Dakota, I've got to get down there and look for Joe. And before I can do it I have to be able to see what I'm doing. Any ideas?"

Dakota gave Wheeler one of those wistful looks, the kind that only those connected at the heart would understand. With his tail wagging, he turned several times toward one of the lone objects that hadn't disappeared into the abyss. Barking several times toward Wheeler he understood that he wasn't getting the message. Moving toward the object he picked up the handle of the paint box and moved toward his friend, finally dropping the object at Wheeler's side.

"Thanks boy but there's nothing left to paint. The canvas jumped ship along with the brushes and a lot of the paints. And for some reason I don't see a lot of beauty around me at the moment."

They just looked at each other, neither moving. And then a light went on in Wheeler's head. He reached over and opened the paint box and smiling, pulled out a small flashlight. Grabbing Dakota and wrestling with him for a moment his friend knew Wheeler was thankful for the idea. He turned it on to make sure it worked and then crawled back over to the edge.

A quarter of his body now hung suspended over what he momentarily thought might be the beginning of a new miniature Grand Canyon. Slowly the beam of light began to find its way across the darkness, every now and then managing to land on something but yet finding nothing. He moved it from side to side, up and down and every which way he could. Out from the side was a small jutting mound of dirt, forming an inverted pyramid. On its top, barely balanced, lay Darby's saddle. Unfortunately, it was just out of reach. Finally Wheeler moved the light under himself. What he saw confirmed what he had felt just a short time ago and caused him to jerk his head back up and his eyes to momentarily close, his way of dismissing it.

Another tremor, something like an aftershock, moved through his body. What his light disclosed was that his entire body was laying on a ledge that was no thicker than several inches at best. Everything inside him went numb. But when finally, the electrical impulses of thought shot through his mind once again, he instinctively knew that it was supporting him, strange as it might be. A third time now his body forged forward, making its way over the side, into that region of the ethers referred to as the abyss.

This time the light went back beyond him as far as it could. He discovered that the several inch thickness he was laying on had extended itself almost twice his length below him and was far wider than he could ever have imagined. But there was a small ledge he hadn't seen before, set back a number of feet from the point where the mantle began to thicken. And then it looked like the opening of what he could only describe as a cave. The question was, how was he going to get down there.

"What is it that you fear? For you are God incarnate. You create what you choose to see and experience in all aspects of life. You can never be harmed for you are an infinite being only momentarily sheathed in a physical body. As such, time stands still for you and you move only within its limited frame of reference. But you always remain who you are in your truest form. You are connected to All That Is, just as All That Is is connected to each and every aspect of itself. You, connected to you, connected to others in the same way. An omnipotent being. What is it that you fear?"

She read the passage over and over again. And it somehow calmed her. Somehow gave her back to herself. And with the continuing miles, the vision of the quake became less and less of a concern, a knowingness growing within her that everything would turn out all right. Wheeler and Simple Joe would somehow be okay. The earth had moved and the vacuum had lifted, allowing the sound of the sliding plates to momentarily displace a solid fixture. But it would be okay.

July continued to move over the land at the speed of a diving hawk, focused so clearly on her destination, on the two men foremost in her life. The State sign she passed in a blur said leaving Texas. The one that followed said welcome to New Mexico. Several hours later she manipulated the corner of that State and was heading north through Pueblo, Colorado. A long time on the road but she was holding up, focused on what mattered most to her. She could still go for awhile without a rest. Or so she thought.

About two hundred miles from the Wyoming border she hit the wall. That invisible shield that turns the forces of nature against you. As you approach it you can begin to feel it in your body. It doesn't matter whether you're walking, running or driving. The internal body clock that's so much a part of this reality is beginning to shut down, signaling to you that it's had enough for now.

Her eyes closed for the tenth time in five minutes, this time remaining closed. She went deep, visions flashing before her at an unheard of speed. Her face contorted and then pulled back. Sadness and pity combined. She shook her head, trying to shake the scene, unable to comprehend what she was seeing. And then her face relaxed, finally accepting what was unfolding before her. Glass shields, each in their own. They were moving toward her. No. She was moving toward them. Wheeler and Simple Joe. Wheeler was reaching out to her, his arm moving through the flexible shield yet still contained within it. She was miles away yet she knew that a step in the right direction, one single step, would allow her to reach out and touch him. Simple Joe was moving toward her. No. He was also moving toward Wheeler. Another step and he'd be there too, but he was moving so very slow. She attempted to call out to both of them but nothing was coming out. Simple Joe mouthed something to her but she couldn't make it out. And then, she felt someone hit her on the head . . .

For the length of a hundred yards the car continued to move in a straight line. And then it didn't. Within seconds it was moving over a dirt lined field of nothing but open space. At a speed of over eighty miles an hour the bottom of the car grazed weeds and caught small pebbles thrown at it from the under-spin of the front tires. Bouncing into and then out of small crevices before being guided over miniature mounds, made both by nature's recent rainfall and some furry animal's movement beneath the ground, her car seemed to follow an erratic path of an unseen rail trestle.

Finally July was jarred awake by the simultaneous actions of a voice yelling at her to wake up and take control, and the car's tires hitting a dirt mogul causing her to hit her head on the roof of the inside of the vehicle. July's eyes instantly took in what was happening. Involuntarily her foot found the brake pedal and shoved it to the floor. Her hands, now firmly gripping the steering wheel, tried with desperation to negotiate a path for the car off of the invisible trestle. At times screaming and at others swearing, she moved into her pace and in less than half a minute had everything under control, slowly bringing the car to a stop.

Getting out of the car, walking around it and at times kicking the tires, she really laid into herself. "God, are you nuts or what? Of all the stupid things you've done, this one is up there at the top of the list. Ouch! Jesus that damn thing's hard." Finding her foot and gently massaging her toes she began to settle down somewhat. "I'm so exhausted I'm not paying attention any longer. I've got to sit back and rest awhile. A catnap. Just a catnap.

Chapter Nineteen

Wheeler's torso was almost entirely suspended over the ledge, his lower body flat against the ground on top. In his long underwear, one pant leg tied around his right ankle, the other around a small, very thin tree stump that he had once laid his paintbrush on, he had creatively given himself the extra length needed to attempt to reach the saddle.

His fingers were now missing it by inches, his mind always aware of the thin layer of earth he lay on, and how at any time the decision by Mother Earth might be made not to sustain his weight, dropping him if he was lucky at the cave's entrance, if not, into the depths of blackness and what lay in its grasp.

"Ugh! God, I'm close. Com'on, just a little bit further."

He knew he was stretched to his limit and that anything could give way at any moment, but he was too far to quit now. Reaching his hand in the opposite direction he touched the underbelly of the ledge and pushed on it to give himself swing. With that accomplished he returned to the targeted saddle, reaching with all his might, catching the horn on the first pass. The jeans were supporting the extra weight.

Using every muscle in his body, those he knew he had and those he was just now becoming aware of, he pulled with all his might to raise both himself and the saddle. His body now completely flat, half on and half off the ledge, he inched backwards until only the saddle remained to be pulled onto the earth.

Panting and sweating he released the saddle on top of the ledge. It took him a moment to catch his breath, every muscle in his body telling him just how much he hurt. In time he reached for one of the attached saddlebags and opened it. "Shit, it's empty!" Before reaching for the other one he looked to the sky and said a silent prayer. It looked bigger than the empty one so there was hope. His hand hit pay dirt. Out from the bag came a small thin rope, it's twenty-five foot length wound so tightly it looked like no more than five feet. Disappointed at first, as he unwound it he inwardly nodded, knowing that he had been right to try for the saddle, that this would get him to the entrance of the cave below him and possibly to Joe.

She walked around the car talking to herself, not sure of just why she felt as frustrated and eager as she did, knowing that there was still a ways to go. "Four hours I slept, four hours. That was one hell of a catnap July, one hell of a catnap."

She pulled out the map and looked it over. Finding her route, knowing she still had hundreds of miles to go, she let out a frustrated sigh. Taking a final walk around the car she folded it up and threw both it and herself back onto the front seat. In moments she was back on the road, racing toward Wheeler and Simple Joe.

It took awhile and a stop for gas in Casper but she was once again focused on what was happening. Every now and then a mental picture of a man without clothes, suspended and dangling from a spider's silky string would flash before her. She'd see him reaching for something but not being able to reach it, and she knew what he knew. That the thin line of silk suspending him could break at any moment and he would be lost. The vision both terrified her and made her laugh. She felt guilt, not understanding why, until she remembered the passage . . .

"What is it that you fear? For you are God . . . You, connected to you, connected to others in the same way. An omnipotent being. What is it that you fear?"

The passage was an important part of this trip. It was always there for her when it was needed. And during the trip she would read it to herself many times for comfort.

He had waited twenty minutes after retrieving the saddle before attempting the cave. First to regain his strength and secondly to build his spirit. He had tried closing his eyes, focusing on Simple Joe, sensing, feeling, trying to make some kind of contract with his inner wisdom, searching for any and all help offered. Nothing had come to him but silence. He tried leaning over the edge and calling to him again.

"Joe, it's Wheeler, are you there? Say something, anything. If you can't talk maybe you can find a pebble on the ground next to you and toss it against something. It would sure help if I could hear that you're down there. If not a pebble, maybe you could remove a boot or something. Anything, just some kind of a sign. Joe!?"

He was angry at himself for feeling so incapable at the moment, so impotent. He tried again to close his eyes and focus. This time what he got shocked him. He saw July, flying over the ground at an uncontrollable speed, not aware of what was happening. Before he opened his eyes he remembered mentally calling out to her to wake up and take control.

He shook the image from his mind, knowing he had to concentrate on the task before him. Still in his underwear, once again trusting the jeans for additional length and support, he had taken the rope and tied the tightest knot he knew how around the exposed leg of the jeans, the other leg still tied around the small thin ground stump. On the other end of the rope he tied a loop knot, and then moved the knot down to the size of a hand circle, knowing he would be able to enlarge it to fit around his waist if an emergency arose. He

Jeff Gutterman

knew if he had tied it around himself, which would have been the safest way to go, he may be passing up the several additional feet he needed to swing over to the cave's entrance. With that, as gently and easily as he could, he fit his hand through the loose circle and then tossed the remaining twenty or so feet of the rope into the air and over the side, watching it fall to invisibility below him.

He then began the laborious task of slowly lowering himself over the top of the ledge, holding onto the fibrous cord with all he could muster. Wheeler was a sight. In his long-johns and boots, flashlight in his open mouth clenched between his teeth, a bracelet of very thin, somewhat frayed rope looped around his hand, he looked much like an Indian goddess in drag. Into the depths of nothingness he went, holding tightly, releasing the top hand to a rung below the lower hand, careful and aware of his impressive weight and what it might do to the rope. He had the momentary thought of knowing how a spider felt, suspended by a very thin line, dangling in the air without a net below. And then, glancing downward into the almost pitch blackness, he returned to his purpose. He had a sense of the second ledge almost ten feet down and about fifteen feet above where he needed to be. At the foot of the lower ledge was the entrance to the cave. All was holding and he was very thankful. This wasn't the way he wanted things to end.

First a foot and then two. Slowly, ever so slowly. Long before he knew it should happen, his foot scraped the surface of something solid and scared the bejezus out of him, causing an immediate halt to his destination.

"What in the world . . ."

And then he understood. The inverted mound that the saddle had been suspended upon was his unseen friend. He tried putting some weight on it, only to discover its limitations. He reasoned that he could however, use it as a fulcrum point to begin a swing and faster declination onto the ledge below. The reasoning was short lived. He noticed that he had only used about five feet of the rope and well understood that the ledge lay at least another fifteen to twenty feet below him.

Again he began lowering himself a foot at a time. Six, seven and eight feet. His muscles were beginning to tighten on him. The small flashlight was on but from the way Wheeler was facing, was hitting nothing solid. He had to keep going and he knew it. Nine, ten feet. Lower into the depths. A few more feet and he'd try to shine the light on the cave to see what he could. Hand over hand, slowly racing against time. He knew Joe was in trouble but had no idea what kind. His body ached from the strain of his weight and he knew his hands could lose their grip at any time. A rest would be wonderful but it couldn't be taken, he had to keep going. He was almost at that point when he could begin his swing to drop the few feet to the cave's entrance. The rope only had a few feet left before it reached its full extension. Somewhere between the pangs of necessity and fear he fought to keep going.

A bit of an echo but clear as a bell. Wheeler was making what he knew may be his final statement to himself and he needed to say it out loud. "I'm going to lose this if I don't do it now." And with that he began to move down to the end of the rope with large spacing of hand over hand while at the same time he began shifting his body weight from side to side, creating what swing in the rope he could. At first only an inch or two of sideways movement. Then, by pulling his legs up toward him and then releasing them in an arch he was able to propel his body a foot or so away from center. Then several feet and then, as the momentum of the swing took root, he was moving five or six feet in either direction.

It was working. Right up until the time he began to hear a sound that terrified him. He'd heard it earlier on top of the ledge when he was tying one leg of the jeans around the small stump, and had forced a portion of it over and onto an outstretched limb, sharpened by how it had broken in times past. The sound was of tearing cloth.

The rope moved downward an additional inch beyond its measure. Then a second and third inch gave their blessing. And then, with one final unwilling swing from Wheeler, the tear above was complete and the entire length of the rope, half of Wheeler's jeans attached, began its own descent.

———————

She was finally in Montana, having passed Billings, now heading for Helena and then on to the Wolf Creek area. It wouldn't be long now. She could relax. The bulk of the trip was over and she'd soon be with Wheeler and Simple Joe. Her mind's thoughts were switching gears, moving away from the immediacy of the moment, back over past ground with Wheeler. She was starting to feel the emotion again.

In her mind they were making love. Slow, passionate love. Blending each into the other, over and over again. She could feel him within her, touching every part of her being, exciting her senses, raising her heartbeat to an almost unbearable pleasure, causing her blood to race from one part of her body to another at unimaginable speeds. And then in an instant, the feeling of being underwater with the ability to move freely in any direction. Each with blinded sight, intuitively knowing the goal that lay before them, both choosing to break the surface at the same time, releasing the essence of stored and immutable energy, each into the other. For a moment she closed her eyes and savored the feeling. She had been with him again, if only in her mind. And she'd be with him once more if she could continue to focus on the road ahead of her.

Stomach pangs. Mild, but sharp enough to realize, actually for the first time, that she hadn't eaten in quite awhile, and the sandwiches she had left were now gone. About fifty miles outside Billings she spotted a sign that read, *"Country Kitchen, three miles, an Emotional Feast for the Senses. Always Open. Use Invisible exit."* In smaller letters at the bottom of the sign, magnified in bold, were the words, *"The best food in town because your heart's desire helps create it."*

"God that looks good. I can smell the buttermilk biscuits and taste the honeybutter. Maybe a bowl of soup with some vegetable mixed in, or better yet, a bisque of some kind. What am I doing? I'm making myself salivate."

Knowing how the mileage indicators on road signs aren't always accurate, she began to slow as she approached what she thought the two mile mark might be, thinking of herself a little like an Eagle, diving to get a closer look at its pray before gliding silently toward it for lunch. At three miles she slowed even further, thinking the country kitchen that put the sign there knew just what they were talking about, and the exactness of distance of their own café. But so far, nothing. At four miles she was crawling, now thinking she had missed it altogether. Turning around she started back down the highway at a mild jog, tires turning no more than a few miles an hour. She was too hungry to miss the turnoff. By the time she had returned to the spot where she had first noticed the sign she was frustrated.

"Twice down the road now and twice defeated. Maybe it doesn't exist anymore." Turning the car around once again she started back toward her original destination. Twenty-five feet later she brought it to a screeching halt on the side of the road. Without turning the engine off she set the hand brake and flew from her seat. She started off walking but the anticipation was too much and she ended up running back toward the sign. She turned and stopped on a dime when she reached it. Mouthing the words aloud, hesitating with long pauses and a trace of tears she read, *"Country Kitchen, three miles, an Emotional Feast for the Senses. Always Open. Use Invisible exit. The best food in town because your heart's desire helps create it."*

Reading it again and again she began shaking her head in understanding as though partially getting it but failing miserably in her ability to capture its complete essence. "My imagination's working overtime . . . It's not that easy. It can't be." She sat where she stood, exchanging glances between the sign and the ground, occasionally looking in an upward direction for some sign from the invisible heavens. Nothing but space and silence. And for an ever so gentle moment her own mind reached that impossible stage of quiet. No fleeting thoughts, one into the other. But it didn't last. An inner explosion of her past meetings with Wheeler engulfed her. And in a moment she knew and understood. All of it. Every last bit of it. How it happened. Why it happened. The cause. The result. The past. The present. At a thousand miles a second it ran through her mind. She was indeed a God. She understood how it worked, and how it didn't. And then, as quick as it had come, it was gone.

July

What she had gained in knowledge she had lost in a memory made of mist.

He landed with a thud. A loud thud. He had fallen miles, traveled for days through the blackness, all within seconds. In his descent he had made peace with his devils and thanked his gods. What more could he do. He'd said goodbye to July and Simple Joe, shouted for Dakota and saw a lifetime pass before him. All that he knew, he knew was disappearing. Dust to dust and all that stuff. Until the loud thud. And now he was in the middle of what, he didn't know. Nothing to explain it because he couldn't see anything. Lying on something hard, afraid to move, knowing his mind was alive but not wanting to venture further.

He remembered passing through layers of glass. Not hard and brittle but malleable. Hitting each individual sheet, and there must have been hundreds, he re-played each contact, not immediately going through each piece but rather into its mix of rich components, and then stretching it to its limit before breaking out the other side and moving onto the next for an identical experience.

It was like making contact with, and then moving through, a plastic wrap of some kind. Imaginings of the mind. There was no other explanation.

He moved his hand and could feel a light air current between his fingers. No pain. The bones were okay. Without lifting it, he managed to slide his arm closer to his body. The body he couldn't feel. Then the other arm. They both worked. A leg moved and inadvertently touched his other leg which he felt. "Okay, the arms and legs seem to work. No broken bones or I'd feel it by now. Let's try a big one," and with that, lifted his head and turned it from first to the left and then to the right. "Movement with no pain. So far, everything works."

Trying to sit up didn't prove as easy for Wheeler. He was sore. His entire back area, from the bottom of his tailbone to the top of his neck. Everything hurt. But it all worked and that was the important thing. He tried standing up but fell the first time. His legs just wouldn't support his weight. Trying a second time he had more luck. But it seemed to be short-lived. Taking a step in a direction he knew nothing about, he ran into his mental plastic wrap. Being able to see the invisible mesh and running into it was one thing. Surrounded with the darkness of a thousand nights and running into it was another.

Involuntarily his body jerked backward in fear only to be engulfed by another wall of wrap. Another involuntary jerk. In a matter of seconds Wheeler was like an uncontrollable bouncing ball moving only inches within his confinement.

For the first time in his life he was really frightened, and because of his fear it took longer for him to calm down enough to think. More than anything it was anger that made him regain control. Control enough to remain still. In a moment he realized that the walls of film he had been moving into weren't sticking to him as he moved away from them. It formed a complete cover over the area of his body that it touched, but remained within its own integrity when he backed away from it. He knew now that what he had experienced, his fall into the abyss and his passage through the malleable glass sheets, had been real. And as the idea pushed its way into the recesses of his thought process, his attention turned to what he could only describe as a phasing in and phasing out of July's voice, bouncing from one side of his head to the other. *". . . Emotional Feast for the Senses. Always Open. Use Invisible exit. The best food in town because your heart's desire helps create it."*

Chapter Twenty

Simple Joe was in a very strange place indeed. He wasn't here and he wasn't there. And yet he was. But in a way he understood it. Wheeler on the other hand was in an even stranger place because he couldn't see it to understand it. July's arena had just begun to unravel, all except for a fleeting moment that she had a glimpse of the knowing within it. Then the wall of cloud cover that caused her to lose it, descended once again. Each in their own way, they all wondered what was going on.

Jeff Gutterman

Simple Joe could still hear her words, distant though they were, from another time, now in a much different land. "We're all connected. Both from times past and those infinite futures we dream for ourselves. We've shared each other's space and time and will continue to, although the relationships and identities between us are always fluid and changing. I love you now as I loved you then, and am as much a part of you now as I know I am in the future we're currently living, in some distant space, in some unknown reality."

He remembered her gently. His daughter. Taken from life at July's age. And whenever he focused on her, or at times even July, he realized all over again just how much he missed her warmth and the shared intimacy of father and daughter. He made his way to the hill country and Wheeler because he had wanted to help July. Nothing had been said by Joe, but many years ago, after his daughter had passed the physical plane, the fading in and out that July had been experiencing with Wheeler, he had also experienced with his daughter. He thought it had happened because of desire but knew there was more than that. For even with a desire to be with each other, when it happened, they couldn't hold their time together for very long. There were fleeting moments at best and that was heartbreaking. A separation that you were trying to put to rest but was being kept alive. But only for moments. Watching July's reaction each time she was pulled away from Wheeler, he now thought he had the missing piece of the puzzle.

July was back on the road to Helena. The Wolf Creek area was only a stone's throw from there. Her mind kept floating between thoughts of life with Wheeler before she left, and her relationship with Simple Joe after him. She loved both of them, each in their own way. Sam Wheeler was the man in her life. Always would be. Simple Joe was the father figure she remembered and had missed greatly. They both had a piece of her heart.

The rush was over, the long flight now somewhat quieting, her car moving down the highway at a much slower pace. There was something settling within her, making her less anxious. A double-edged sword of sorts, the knowing coming back in its own way, while the mist continued to hold its ground. Changes were in the air. She found herself beginning to float, the same feeling she remembered just before she found herself in the cabin with Wheeler.

"All right. What's going on. This isn't funny. I'm getting lightheaded again, like something is passing through me, some invisible . . ." She hit the brakes as quickly as she could while at the same time turning the wheel of the car off the main highway, bringing it to a screeching halt less than ten feet in front of one of the most beautiful horses she had ever seen. The horse held his position. Removing herself from the car she approached this great stallion. Still he didn't move. Fear was not part of who he was. As she approached, he bowed his head, his long mane slapping the air. He was big and powerful, his legs trimmed with a multicolored whirling mix of golden wheat that extended up from his ankle area and flowed into an antique white, both above and below it. With the dirt road below him and the mountains behind him, he looked to July as though he was floating above the ground. The sound of his name came from an unknown sense deep within her. Reaching out to touch him the unfamiliar word of "Fortune" left her lips. She didn't know how nor why, just that the name was his.

He was wild, free, yet he allowed her to mount. From that moment on they became one, each knowing the other, each sensing where they were to go. Holding tight to his mane they moved, slowly at first to allow her to adjust. Then to a soft gallop and finally to the air and that undiscernibly narrow path that she was meant to follow. The road left behind her now in a memory, the air thin, the mist continuing to surround her every thought. She was going to Wheeler, she knew it. It was going to happen again. And she wanted it. She had prayed for it. Over and over once again. She knew now what Wheeler had felt when Stanley had lifted into the air. Her heart was racing. Beating at a rate she thought impossible. And then it seemed it wasn't beating at all. She wasn't losing her presence as she had in the past. She was fully awake and taking in every single movement.

Flying faster than she could calculate they seemed to enter a wormhole, moving through its translucent walls, twisting and turning without touching its sides. The colors of the wormhole were astonishingly brilliant, as they floated by and changed on her an unlimited number of times. It widened, it narrowed, it split as they approached a fork. July had a momentary jolt as Fortune took both routes at the same time, for a fraction of a second a portion of herself seeming to split into two separate entities as he had done. But she wasn't lessened in any way. Rather she was whole and complete in both identities. The thought of what was happening took a time span of a millionth of a second, a billionth of a second quicker than their coming together again as just one horse and rider.

Their speed seemed to increase and then they shot out into what appeared to be nothingness. She was only aware for a fraction of a thought before everything disappeared from her view, "Fortune" included, and once again she entered that peace-like space that only the sleep of a baby enjoys.

The voice had silenced him before he wept. Her voice had come to him so clear, the emotion had returned with a rush. To the Gods of Stillness he cried over and over again. "July, where are you?" And then the silence filled the air around him, seemingly for a lifetime. Wheeler knew he had entered hell. He would spend an eternity in darkness, occasionally hearing her voice, feeling her presence without the contact. His hope had run its course. He was finally defeated. Totally and completely. But the human heart lives on in hope and his was no different. This time the voice he heard wasn't in his head.

"Wheeler, where are you?"

For a moment he didn't respond. How could he. She wasn't really here. He'd simply be talking to himself. Insane, yes. Crazy, yes. Plain nuts, he was sure of it. But then he heard her again, this time loud and clear.

"Wheeler, I know you're here."

Silence, disbelief. And then a comment that had been made to him long ago came forth in a rush. Not a voice so much as being able to picture the words themselves: "The gold will always be found in the darkness." His eyes grew in size with his excitement. And then the words gushed from his mouth. "July . . . am I hearing right?"

"My God Wheeler, it is you. Where are you?"

"Where am I? I'm . . . I'm wrapped up like a sandwich. Where are you?"

"I . . . I don't know. I can't see anything. I don't know."

"You've got to come to me. I can't move more than a couple of feet in any direction."

"How can I come to you when I can't see you?"

Then they both heard it. An answer to her query. Fortune's simple neigh. He knew the sound, but it was July who smiled. Just as he had supported her so far, the white Stallion would continue to carry her to Wheeler. She started to tell him to call out her name, to keep calling until Fortune could pick up the direction of his voice, but the words didn't come quickly enough.

A loud rumbling. A moving. A tearing of sorts. The earth going through its birth cycle again, regenerating itself. Rock n' Roll was the name of the tune. Everything started to shake. Their voices attempting to reach out to each other were lost in the energy of the ethers.

Both were in a darkness of sorts. Wheeler in his saran wrap without the benefit of light or space, while July, still mounted on Fortune, tried to move silently through a waking mist of rumbling ground. While the earth continued to share its music, Wheeler remained captive while July and Fortune slowly made their way through an invisible passage without the benefit of noticeable landmarks. A few feet, several yards, a block, the thunderous noise continued while they moved. Although a time since they'd been together, both Wheeler and July's inner bodies made the length of incredible simultaneous changes, some they were aware of, others on a level they would never know about. They had finally connected again, yet they were unable to touch physically. They were close in proximity to one another, but they weren't. The verbal exchange they had established had been lost in the imperceptible distance of rolling sound and movement. The swell and release of everything around them momentarily put a hold on any sort of union between them.

Minutes passed that suggested hours had moved through their space. To block the fury they both played their independent mind games of fantasy. Each with the other in a different space, comfortable, loving and complete. Imagination had taken over, pulling them away from their fear and longing. Away from the immediate excitement of the moment. Suddenly July felt the firmness beneath Fortune beginning to dissolve again. Downward they moved, deeper and deeper into the abyss, July's arms around Fortune's disappearing neck, screaming all the way.

Wheeler was frozen, unable to move. The saran wrap, the fear, it didn't matter, he couldn't move, every inch of him in complete paralysis. He heard her screams over the rumbling and movement of the earth but couldn't help her. The frustration, the shame of his inability to act. His only movement was a tiny trinket of tears making their way down his face at the speed of a rushing river.

Simple Joe's new space was well-lighted, although he didn't understand just how. There was no above to shine down and nothing glowing from within. Speculation was unprofitable. He had heard the two of them talking just before the earth began to move again. And then he had heard her fear, loud and piercing. On some level he felt that the earth was digesting the energy that was causing it all. An energy that he now knew both Wheeler and July were creating, even if they didn't. This was the chosen area to confront their invisible thoughts, their coming together and releasing, over and over again.

He was comforted by his sense that July was close. Without knowing she'd come, he knew she'd be with him at the right time. Contradictions with an inward knowing. Always. Moving from his stable of thoughts he glanced around the space he shared with a not altogether unfamiliar energy. Where exactly was he, he wondered. There were no walls, nothing concrete he could call a foundation, no covering to the space at all. A magical area without boundaries.

And then he understood. And in that moment, that split second, that time period within him that allowed a million atoms to flicker on and off at a speed completely incomprehensible to the human mind, granting only illusion to our solidity, his overall sense of reality as he knew it was shattered forever. And at the same millisecond the knowing came to him, his love for his friends rode the distance of belief systems, offering it to them.

Wheeler's saran shields began to vibrate at the same moment Simple Joe's thoughts reached him. Although the saran remained, it appeared that something was finally starting to happen. Continuing for several minutes before finally returning to normal, these invisible vibrations caused the shields to pulsate with life, a rainbow of colors of all hues fluttering for position within their domain, while always in a continuous flow. The very moment he allowed understanding in and then accepted what he received, the fog lifted and he had a far clearer view of what had occurred than anything he had ever had. The thoughts turned over and over within him, his mind accepting instantly, this idea that came from somewhere deep within him. It was simple yet so powerful. "This has all been symbolic. There are no boundaries in reality except those we give ourselves with our thoughts. We create for ourselves either limitations or freedoms." He looked around him, grasping just how much he had played a part in bringing this play into the theater of his mind, that of July's and Simple Joe's.

He listened for her but could hear nothing. And then he called out.

"July, sweetie, can you hear me?" Nothing. Empty unimpassioned movement of the air surrounding him.

"Simple Joe, can you hear me?" A repeat of nothing. Furls of energy passing through the linked space of neighboring molecules.

He felt he was becoming free, yet frustration remained within him. But it was that anger at possible defeat that caused a simple plan to surface. He would write a new script, created first in his minds eye and then thrust out into reality. He didn't know whether those in the unidentified ethers needed to share his vision for it to work. But he knew if they had knowledge of his idea it would make it stronger.

"July, I think you can hear me but can't respond for some reason. And Simple Joe, I'm just hopeful if you can hear me and understand what we're going to try and do. July, sweetie, I want you to listen to me. I'm going to try something. I'm going to try sending some thoughts out to you. A communication of sorts. But it's more than that. I'm going to let that aspect of my knowing guide what happens, what's said. If I'm right, you'll feel it, be a part of it. We'll be doing it together, and, if I'm right, we can come together again. Here goes. First, relax, draw a few breaths . . . Now, try and clear your mind from where you are, from what's going on. Concentrate on empty space, nothingness. Sweetie, I hope you can hear me. We're doing this together, you and me. Concentrate . . . Now, begin to form a picture of the two of us in your mind, but do it away from this place . . . Our cabin, think of our cabin and the two of us there. Just with each other. Simple, keep it simple, at least for now. Concentrate sweetie, concentrate . . ."

With all his might he kept telling himself he could do this. For all of them. "No limitations this time Wheeler, none. But opened-ended, granting choice. This time with the wisdom to create the right one. Come on boy, concentrate. Concentrate." He sat where he had stood and breathed deeply. In his mind's eye he created a scenario of coming together again, all three of them.

Simple Joe was responding just a moment before either Wheeler or July with his visual. He knew how to move from where he was but couldn't. Not just yet. Something was left undone, open, incomplete. It was the energy he'd been feeling in his space. The familiarity of something, someone. That had to be solved before anything else happened. His reason for being in this place had as much to do with him as with Wheeler and July. He'd come to help them but he knew he'd come for himself also.

"I'm here Daddy."

He knew the voice and was immediately forced into mental silence, not daring to let a thought pass through his mind.

"It's okay, it's our time."

Frozen, not a trace of liquid moving over the lens of his eyes. Stillness, like he had never known it. Not fear of hurt but rather fear of losing this new connection.

"I'm not going anywhere. We have the freedom to talk here."

He had to respond but didn't know how. He wanted the connection, had even prayed for it.

"I love you and I'm still a part of you."

"I know. And I love you . . . Can I see you."

"I'll only be able to be seen as long as your heart holds the forgiveness."

In a fraction of a second the gears of his mind began to move. Memories flowed like a river. He worked his mind, moving back in time, allowing his thoughts to lift his mood so he could touch that soft gentle spot of forgiveness within himself. The more focused he became, the more he knew he'd make it. He'd be able to hold the love and the remission. And when he knew it he brought himself forward again, into the present. It took him years to go back through his mind's flight, centuries to re-experience the hurt, eons to understand, and a fraction of a second to forgive, all of it encompassed in the speed of a single thought, all of it now, where he stood. Simple Joe was feeling whole in a way that he hadn't for years. And now, with an open communication with the daughter that he had lost, he'd become complete. Before his eyes she began to appear.

Chapter Twenty-one

With all the validity of his knowing, Wheeler continued to paint an inner landscape. A theater of the mind, written on the wings of spontaneity in an old familiar setting. By focusing on that illusionary monocle within his mind's eye, he began to see himself as he sat on their bed, facing the window that Wildfire had once looked into, granting witness to their lovemaking, their tender embrace of love. Some additional strokes of the brush and she sat next to him, each now touching the other, excited by their reunion. They'd been given another chance. The possibilities hadn't been taken from them after all. They were back in the cabin, the two of them, Wheeler and July, even if it was only in their mind this time.

The mood was one of silence, neither speaking for fear of breaking the spell. They both understood in very clear terms that this was a gift, and if they failed again to grasp what was necessary, it would be their last time together. They now knew instinctively that fate, brought on by their thoughts and emotions and desires, had lent a hand in this mind coupling. Both had worked hard, experienced much, neither wanting to let go of the emotions that had brought them to this point, once again granting an opportunity for fulfillment and closure, most of all, everlasting love.

Two pair of eyes searched the room for Simple Joe. Slowly they moved from the bed, hand in hand walking into each room, hoping against all hope that Joe hadn't been left behind in the unknown underground reality they had just left. When at last they came to the door of the final room, all others an empty vacuum, there was panic, each heart invisibly reaching beyond itself to their friend. Wheeler reached for the knob, held it for a moment and then began to twist it ever so slowly. In a moment the brass protrusion was free of the door jamb. All he had to do now was push inward and they could walk into the room. But he didn't. In what seemed like an hour to July, the granite statue

that Wheeler had become made no overt movement to complete the search. Instead, he simply
loosened his grip on the doorknob, forcing the
brass outgrowth back into its familiar space, and
eventually withdrew his hand without opening it.

As he released the doorknob he turned from
the door. Looking deeply into July's eyes he hesi-
tated for a moment and repeated the same words
to her that had been forming in her mind for the
last several minutes. "I'm getting the feeling that
he's not supposed to be here. This cabin wasn't
part of his life."

"He's okay Wheeler. I just know it. Somehow
I can sense it. I can feel it."

"I think you're right. But I don't know that
we'll see him again. What happened to us . . .
happened to all of us. There are connections that
will always hold us in a pattern, a relationship to
each other. You and I were there for each other. I
think Joe was there initially to help both of us
understand . . . first with you and then here with
me to offer what he could, maybe some additional
pieces of the puzzle of why you and I keep
finding each other and then getting pulled apart
again. To make sense of it all. But he also had his
own agenda, something that was probably
unknown to him at a level he could consciously
retain it."

"I know. I've been thinking the same thing. For us, the love and the fear have been like a tug of war. I think it's the same for Simple Joe. I remember him saying something about his daughter. How close they were and how much he loved her when she was alive. And then how much he felt he had blamed her when his wife had left him, and how he couldn't forgive himself for that and then later for dying. It was very disturbing to him. Kept him wrapped up most of the time in guilt and shame over his own thought process. I think that's why he wanted to help me so much."

"I'm not sure I'm following you there."

"He had told me how much I reminded him of his daughter. With me he had the love, without the burden of his lack of forgiveness."

"Like us, there's something they need to settle. Actually, Simple Joe needs to settle. One time he alluded to the two of them almost seeing each other after she had died. But he gave me the feeling it wasn't something solid, something he could touch. And I think that like us, they're in a position where they've been given a chance to move toward and encompass only the love of the relationship and let go of the hurt forever."

Still holding mental hands, now silent, their eyes traced each others features as they had done a thousand times in the past. Without words they were moving into the knowing. Simple Joe's pain had had the affect of allowing them to articulate their own.

Unknown hours passed, time played backwards, condensed and stretched at the same moment. They lay in each other's arms, gazing into the face of the other, committed as two sources of mind energy could ever be. Hand and fingertips gently moved over the others body, tracing and retracing the outlines they both knew so well. Touching and being touched, kissing and being kissed, gently, easily. Wheeler brushed July's hair with his eyes while his hands massaged the small of her back. Relaxing and exciting in the same movement.

"Wheeler, I love you. More and more each time we're together."

The kidding smirk came immediately, "I know."

For revenge, she reached out and tweaked his nipple, causing his mental body to momentarily jerk, a physical response, a small yelp escaping from his throat.

"So that's how we're going to play the game!" He reached for her but wasn't fast enough, July already having anticipated his response by covering her breasts.

They rolled and played from one end of the bed to the other and then began again. The sky changed colors a hundred times and grass seedlings became a golden meadow. Nothing, but nothing, was going to separate them this time.

When it was time, before exhaustion set in, they talked of why and how, of times before and future times. She led, he followed, and then they reversed their verbal expressions. They fenced, they danced, they came together, they momentarily separated and then came together again, this time a stronger appearance of connection.

Wheeler was alive with feeling, July's excitement moving through him the more they talked, broken now only by a hollow cry from within the physical realms of their fortress. Without forethought or movement, Wheeler immediately opened his eyes and broke their mental dance.

"Can anyone hear me?"

Wheeler moved his head and rolled his eyes, trying to focus on the familiar voice. But long before he found his own, he heard another.

"Joe is that you? Yes, yes, I can hear you."

"July?"

"I'm here Joe."

"And Wheeler?"

"We're both here Joe, but where are you?"

"I'm . . . I'm not sure."

"Are you hurt in any way?"

"No, no, not at all. As a matter of fact, wherever I am, well, it's the best thing that could've happened to me."

"What are you talking about?"

"You wouldn't believe me if I told you."

"Try us."

"Well, okay . . . I'm with my daughter."

In a mysterious cavern under a mountaintop where games of all kinds were played, there was stillness and silence. In over an hour they hadn't heard Simple Joe's voice. But during that hour, ever so slowly, the magic continued to happen. Wheeler saw it first, looking off into a blackened, uncalculated distance, a haze of light was beginning to appear. Walking toward him was July, slowly and sure footed. Obscured but as beautiful as ever, she looked ethereal. When she was within a few feet of his plastic prison, he knew why. July's essence was also surrounded by a thin sheet of saran wrap.

Now it was her turn. As she continued to move she was able to focus on him. Eye to eye for the first time in a long time. They had traded on each other's thoughts and because of that had once again been granted an aspect of the physical. But this was a little different and they both knew it. Seeing each other for the first time in many months, each wrapped as a sandwich, made both of them tear, smile, and then laugh.

Wheeler was the first to speak. "It's a slow process but I think we're doing okay?"

"I think we're doing great. But I am a little concerned."

"I can't imagine why." Attempting to move his arm out beyond the saran in front of him was a mistake. Frustration immediately found its psychological mark.

"How come I can move and you can't?"

"Good question. Can I add where are we, and why are we wrapped like mummies, and more than any of that, where's here?"

"Can you feel it?"

"Sweetie, what are you talking about?" Wheeler moved from one corner of his space to the other. Stopping at his see-through wall, he looked straight at July. Those gorgeous dark green eyes of hers warmed his essence and he couldn't imagine what she was referring to. Then something unusual, something known yet unknown, suddenly grabbed hold of him and chilled him to the bone. Whatever she had caught scent of, he was now feeling it too. Something invisible, something not there. They'd both sensed it before, several times before, usually several minutes before they were pulled from each other's life again.

She took the final step into Wheeler, surprisingly leaving her sheathed prison behind as she moved into his. They were still somewhere in the unknown, but there was no longer anything between them. No division of any kind. They could actually touch. Wheeler was stunned that July could just walk to him, so stunned that he didn't move.

"If you don't immediately put your arms around me, I'm leaving."

Laughing he reached out and picked her up, surrounding her with his long, still somewhat tired arms. They waited. Nothing more than what they felt initially. No enhanced presence this time.

Only something making itself known. Energy, a force, something.

"Wheeler, what's going on?"

"I think . . . it's a warning. That's all."

"Why?"

"Sweetie, I'm almost positive that this isn't something separate from us. I think we created it. Our thoughts have created it. Our beliefs are both very strong. There's a lot of energy behind what we've put out. It's not going to let us go until we deal with all of it."

July dropped her head into his chest, tears filling her eyes. "I'm afraid to get much deeper than we have. I think that if this energy we've created doesn't pull us apart again, moving into it to explore our own quiet thoughts just might."

"I know. I've had the same feeling. But I think if we try, and we succeed, we have a chance of staying together. What's happening now is a warning that we need to complete something if we're going to make this reunion permanent, something we haven't touched on yet. We're together. The way I look at it, we're making progress. If we give up and let the fear of pushing each other away with our most intimate thoughts win, well, we'll have defeated ourselves, and we'll be separated again anyway, and probably sooner than later."

Chapter Twenty-two

They were both still deep within the earth's crust and they knew it. This fear that constantly lived with them came masked as excitement turned upside down and inside out. From it could spring eternal life. It could be pleasant or hopeless. The choice was theirs. Continued frustration and hopelessness would be their gift if they discounted the concentric motives that kept causing their separation. They needed to move away from their fear of disconnection. And that could only be accomplished by confronting their demons and moving through them. These shadows that had played with their togetherness during their relationship.

They wanted so badly to stay together this time, even in this unknown reality. So, in one final attempt to understand, once again they began to review their relationship, this time where initial actions and reactions had created thoughts of separation and fear. The good times were easy to cover, and they were included when the air around them began to attract its heavy currents. From the time they first met, to the time they first became separated, each in their own way, they talked about those thoughts and ideas that had occurred to both, but had been pushed to the back of their minds without expression.

They talked until exhaustion set in and then talked some more, neither letting up, neither willing to see what they had together disappear again. After several hours their voices were trailing well behind their thoughts, their senses becoming dull and their limbs weathering in pleasant numbness. But a second wind blew in from the heavens and filled their unknown reality, allowing them to continue, a regeneration for their inner selves and what had to be said.

With a raspy voice Wheeler continued. "Sweetie, we need to be so very clear on what we're saying. Everything out, no misunderstandings. This is an opportunity for both of us to change the decisions that separated us to begin with. An opportunity to forgive ourselves and each other."

July was focused, clear in her thoughts. "Wheeler, for both of us, it just keeps coming back to trust and faith. Maybe more defined now than when we talked at the cabin the last time we were there when all this started again. More so than even a few minutes ago."

"What do you mean?"

"A couple of things. I tried so hard not to love you, not to be in love with you when I left. I think now I understand that love really is a state of mind and that state of mind is dependent on our perception. Do you remember when I said that I left because I didn't believe you loved me, that you never said anything. And how important that was to me?"

"Yes."

"I meant what I said, but yet I need to acknowledge something. Something I may not have spoken before. It's simply this. I know in my heart how considerate and generous you were in everything between us, especially yourself. In your way, you were showing me how much you loved me. The picture's much clearer now than it was back then. I'm sorry if I'm a slow learner. It affected both of us. I wanted love. I had asked for it and I had prayed for it. And with you I got it.

Your sweet love. I needed to look at what was happening more than what was or wasn't being said. I kept focusing on what I thought should have been said. Don't get me wrong, I'm not dismissing the fact that it would have been nice to hear the words, but really, I had everything I wanted when we were together without a word being spoken. I guess the lesson is to understand that we don't necessarily get what we want in the way we want it, but we do get what we want. Each and every time. So, now I've said it."

Wheeler was quiet, focused on what July had offered, not wanting to interrupt, but he knew he would. "Once knew a very wise man who said that 'transformation is only a change in perception.'"

July nodded her head, caught his drift and gave him a little smirk. "For both of us. I can see you much clearer now also! Partly because you shared a part of who you were in your past before us and partly because I can now understand how you could let past situations dictate your actions with me. Your transformation came in understanding that each person, each situation, is different, and has to be handled and dealt with in the present, not the past. Whatever rejections you went through had nothing to do with us. We were in a different space and time . . . And there's something else."

Wheeler wasn't able to say much, just a continual nod of his head, giving July the space to continue with what she was saying.

"There's something I've never talked about very much, maybe because I wasn't able to see what I needed to. But I think Simple Joe's situation has helped me see more and see it clearly."

"I'm not sure I'm following."

"Simple Joe's situation with his daughter. Blaming her for things that weren't her fault, inevitably causing separation."

"You're losing me kiddo."

"Do you remember when I told you about my father dying when I was very young and how it affected me."

"Of course."

"I think what I didn't say, because I truly didn't understand it, was that in a way, I felt that he had abandoned me. I loved him so much and then to have him leave, I never wanted to feel that way again. Never wanted to repeat it. I think subconsciously I was always trying to keep a safe distance from loving someone that much. And the only way I could do that was to keep a safe distance from deep involvement. From you. Even though you were what I wanted, what I had searched for, what I longed for. The longer we were together the closer you got. The closer we got. And it scared me to death. I think I actually started believing that it would happen again. That I would be abandoned. I did a number on myself. And I couldn't tell you about it."

Both of them were tearing, Wheeler's head moving in agreement with July's comments before making one of his own. "Baggage and ghosts. They'll always keep us in a holding pattern. No forward movement. Just the status quo . . . until we're able to release and move on. I think it's about forgiving ourselves and others."

She smiled first and then reached over and hugged him. "Forgiveness. It's one of the keys isn't it? And so very important. Everything is going to continue to happen until we take responsibility for creating what we do, each situation, each interaction. It has to do with accepting responsibility. It's the only way to clear. It's like in a dream. The same scene keeps coming, the same people showing up, until you can identify what they're trying to tell us. Only then do they go away."

Wheeler's brow was furrowing just enough for July to toss a quizzical look back at him. When he didn't respond she playfully punched him in the chest.

"Okay, okay. Just a thought. Suppose, just suppose, that life always exists in its true form. And that before we leave that form and we're born into a physical body, we lay a blueprint, an outline for our life and who we're going to be and what we're going to experience. Not only by ourselves but also what interactions we're going to have with certain others in this lifetime, maybe for the benefit of them, maybe for the benefit of us, or maybe for the benefit of all of us. The blueprint is malleable through choice, laying nothing in concrete. Every situation and person that comes into our lives is flexible, allowing us the experience or not. But always we choose it and always for our mutual benefit. It's like each one of us having a soul code.

"You, me, and Simple Joe."

"Exactly."

"It would make sense."

"Each one of us is getting something from what's been happening. You and I are getting a second chance. Or for that matter maybe even a third and fourth chance the way things have been going for us. In any case, from what you've been telling me, as strange as this sounds, Joe has been able to gain what he's wanted for a long time now. He's now able to work things out with his daughter. He's been given the opportunity to open past wounds and heal them. Heal them permanently for the both of them. For their mutual benefit. That's a second chance after there normally wouldn't be an opportunity for one."

"I just realized something."

"What's that?"

"All this talking we're doing, here and now, and all the things we've already discussed at the cabin. We've really both opened up more than I ever thought was possible."

"I know."

"Do you know that we've talked more about our fears than we ever did when we were together."

"And admitted to a great deal more individual responsibility than we ever have."

"Yes."

They were immobile, staring into each other's eyes as if for the first time. Their thoughts were one, each feeling that it had all been said, everything released. For the present they were drained but energized. A hollow heart was how July would later remember it, filled to the brim until almost bursting.

And then the thickness in the air around them began to change.

Wheeler was about to say something but then turned with July to focus on the saran wrap and watch for the second time as it begin to quiver. A thousand flickers of electricity surging through the air, atoms moving, splitting and then splitting again, trying to hold the form and solidity and trying to let it go, all in the same breath. They held tightly to each other, not knowing quite what to think, if they'd be swept from this unmarked battlefield or forced to stay within it. In the center of the wrap a small hole was beginning to appear, at first only golf ball sized but shortly large enough to move through. They knew it was time to go when rather than increase in size it held its form.

There was hesitation at first but only for a fraction of a second. Taking July's hand in his, Wheeler began to move forward, one small step at a time toward the opening. Only a few feet from where he was standing it took only three steps before he was between and betwixt. His eyes became saucer-like as he stepped through the opening and placed the sole of his boot onto a platform of an invisible solid. More hesitation before he continued. His hand squeezed July's, but she was unaware, focused on Wheeler's boot and his next move.

"Hang tight sweetie. We're about to enter another unknown." Trailing behind him, Wheeler's other leg began to make its approach to go beyond the electrically charged opening, onto the invisible foundation past his other boot. As his leg passed the opening, Wheeler was now in the clear, sweat beginning to trickle down his face. Glancing down it was apparent that he was standing on something, but its mass was invisible to the naked eye. He now forced himself to attempt another step away from the saran and in doing so pulled July with him out onto the magical floor.

Now both were standing on neither knew what. But they were free of the saran wrap. Wheeler looked to the air around them and then at July. "We're free of the limitation we could see, but it seems we've given ourselves another one. One we can't see."

"Or don't want to."

Nodding his head. "Or don't want to."

They both looked around, their visual extending about fifteen feet in any direction with a solid mist beyond that. At exactly the same moment they both echoed the same words for the same question. "Which way and how far?"

I'm going to try something but I'm not going to let you go. If I'm wrong we'll both suffer. If I'm right, we'll have begun our journey out of here."

With July nodding agreement, Wheeler raised his leg to take another step, part of him feeling that it was a step into oblivion, another part of him knowing that all he had learned so far had instinctively taught him to trust himself. As his foot touched down in front of him it caught solid ground, but not before extending itself several inches below the level the majority of his form was on. The discordance threw him and he almost fell forward, taking July with him.

"Have we got this all figured out correctly?"

"Wheeler, I think we've done everything we can do. I'm with you no matter which direction we're going."

Another raised leg, this time perceiving that there would be another step down when his boot hit the ground. He wasn't disappointed. But this time the step down was even lower than the first one. He began shaking his head from side to side, reaching up with his free hand to scratch his head as Simple Joe always seemed to do, and then vocalizing what was in him. "We don't have this all figured out yet. At the rate we're going, a couple more steps and we'll be on a forty-five degree angle to each other, not to mention that I think we're going in the wrong direction."

July was getting a sense of what was happening, a slow smile spreading across her face. "We don't know it's the wrong direction. We're not in a reality that's anything like what we're used to seeing or knowing. I want you to trust me. I think I've got it."

Now it was Wheeler who nodded his head in agreement, smiling as he made his comment to her. "I get it. None of this makes sense. It can't be torn apart and put back together again, not from a logical standpoint at least. Time to put the head to rest and bring the heart into play, huh? I guess that means that it's time for a woman to lead."

Without letting go of each other she just smiled and squeezed his hand as she changed places with him, Wheeler stepping back up the invisible steps and July stepping down into the lead.

"You're going to get us out of here, right?"

"Right. Are you ready?"

"Lead on, McDuff."

And she did, raising her foot enough to step well beyond where she stood and then planting it firmly with expectation. When it was complete she turned to Wheeler and smiled. Not only hadn't she moved below the level at which she stood, but the move was actually somewhat elevated, putting her on the same level with a bewildered Wheeler. But they were now stretched to the limit, neither wanting to let go of the other no matter what direction they moved in. With a gentle tug she pulled Wheeler to her.

He was the first to speak. "The first two steps must have been testing me. It was the third one that was going to start us up and out of here."

"Uh huh. I just learned something that I think is going to be important for both of us."

"If this is a man woman thing I don't want to know about it."

"It is a man woman thing but only as it applies to both of us. It's where our expectation is. That creates our outcome. You weren't sure of where your step would take you. I was."

Wheeler smiled, nodding his head is agreement. And then it happened. The sound and feel of movement. Slow at first, gaining gradually with time. All within the elongated space of a heartbeat. July moved back into Wheeler, his arms encompassing her from behind. At first they sensed forward movement but then as centuries passed they understood they were standing still, only the reality was changing. And then, looking down they saw their legs beginning to be swallowed up in the change, disappearing from the rest of their bodies. Without further warning, the remaining part of their physical essences began to also be consumed by the change. They were both disappearing into the unknown, together.

Epilogue

They stayed together, Wheeler and July, riding Fortune bareback out of a realm that had forced them to cooperate, each with the other for their mutual benefit. No longer two lost souls, one without the other. They had traveled the distance and made the sacrifices necessary. They had opened to each other completely. And in so doing had given in and welcomed the idea of replacing fear with love. In the end they had found each other again, each gaining an understanding and recognition of just how much a part of the other each actually was. Remaining together for the rest of their time would be the easiest part of continuing the circle. Their continued choices would be the most difficult.

Both to the entrance to their property and over the door of their cabin, engraved with golden lettering, they placed two plaques. On the first was etched the following:

> *"Chances and choices are always given.*
> *Opportunities abound. Listen to your heart."*

The second plaque had the following commentary:

> *"Nothing that occurs in life occurs only once. For until we recognize and admit who we truly are, we will be shown again and again and again."*